He was falling for Kristen.

As he watched her sing a lullaby to the tired child, he thought about the first time he'd seen her. She was beautiful, elegant and every inch a woman. But then Fernando remembered the expression on her face when she realized he had taken in six children.

There were many obstacles to overcome: her living in New York, her work there, perhaps even a basic difference in culture. But what if the biggest obstacle was the children?

He had brought her to his home in the hope that when she got to know them she would love them as he did. And now, as he watched Kristen comfort Gretyl, something knotted in his throat. He felt a flare of hope because maybe, after all, there was a chance for both him and his children.

Dear Reader,

It wouldn't be summer without romance, or June without a wedding—and Special Edition brings you both this month!

Our very romantic THAT'S MY BABY! title for June is *Happy Father's Day*, by Barbara Faith. In fact, this daddy has *six* adopted children he calls his own! Now he has to convince the woman of his dreams to become part of his family.

What would June be without blushing brides? Well, first we have book two of Christine Flynn's miniseries, THE WHITAKER BRIDES. In *The Rebel's Bride*, it's renegade Caleb Whitaker's turn to walk down the aisle. And *Waiting at the Altar* is where you'll find ever-faithful Jacob Matthews—this time, he's determined to be a groom at last in book two of Amy Frazier's series, SWEET HOPE WEDDINGS. In Gail Link's *Marriage-To-Be?* the nuptials are still in question—it's up to the bride to choose between two brothers.

Rounding out the month are two authors new to Special Edition. Janis Reams Hudson has a sexy tale in store when two sparring lovers issue the challenge, *Resist Me if You Can*. And after Lois Faye Dyer's *Lonesome Cowboy* meets his match in a spirited schoolteacher, his lonely days just might be over.

So don't miss a moment of these wonderful books. It's just the beginning of a summer filled with love and romance from Special Edition!

Sincerely,

Tara Gavin,
Senior Editor

Please address questions and book requests to:
Silhouette Reader Service
U.S.: 3010 Walden Ave., P.O. Box 1325, Buffalo, NY 14269
Canadian: P.O. Box 609, Fort Erie, Ont. L2A 5X3

BARBARA FAITH

HAPPY FATHER'S DAY

Published by Silhouette Books
America's Publisher of Contemporary Romance

"Oh lovely Spain!
Renown'd romantic land!"
—Byron

 SILHOUETTE BOOKS

ISBN 0-373-24033-3

HAPPY FATHER'S DAY

BARBARA FAITH

is a true romantic who believes that love is a rare and precious gift. She has an endless fascination with the attraction a man and a woman from different cultures and backgrounds have for each other. She considers herself a good example of such an attraction, because she has been happily married for over twenty years to an ex-matador she met when she lived in Mexico.

Dear Reader,

Once in a very rare while a character steps out of the pages of your book and into your heart. So it was for me with Fernando Ibarra, the hero of *Happy Father's Day*.

As he began to emerge he became, for me, a man so vital, so alive, and yes, so passionate, a man of such magnetism and vitality, that I knew I would never forget him.

Fernando has all of the sophistication of a modern-day man, yet there is a rare quality of old-world courtliness and charm about him.

He has a heart full of love, a love he gives to the young American woman who comes into his life. And to so many others, as you will see as you read on.

Southern Spain, land of fairy-tale castles, sunshine and fine wine, seemed the perfect setting for such a man. And this is where the story takes place.

So read on and enjoy. I hope like me, you, too, will fall a little in love with Fernando.

Barbara Faith

Chapter One

Sweat trickled between her breasts, and the sun seeped into her body, melting her bones. Her bones needed melting. So did her brain. Maybe if she stayed out here long enough it, too, would melt.

She looked down at the financial report she'd been studying, but the figures danced and blurred like motes of light, and so instead she looked out at the green waters of the Mediterranean and thought that maybe Tillie had been right about her coming to Spain, after all.

"There's a small hotel in Santa Cruz de la Palma," Tillie had told her. "It's right on the beach, about five miles from Torremolinos. You can swim in the sea, eat Spanish food, drink Spanish wine, and have a fling with whatever good-looking Spanish dude comes your way."

Kristen had never lounged in her life. Nor had she ever taken a real vacation. She wouldn't be here now, if not for Tillie and Dr. Alexander.

"You need a rest, Miss Fielding," the doctor had said. "If you don't take one, you're going to come apart at the seams. Take a month off. Get some sun and try to relax." He'd grinned at Tillie. "Do what Miss McGee says. Have a fling with a Spanish dude."

The word *dude* had sounded strange coming from the lips of the austere Dr. Alexander. She hadn't smiled when he said it, but she smiled now. Both he and her assistant meant well, and yes, although she hated to admit it, she'd known that she needed to get away. She had agreed to come to Spain, but only for a week or ten days, certainly not for a month. As for a Spanish dude, Tillie and the good doctor could forget about that. She'd come alone, and she planned to remain alone. Which was why she'd had a beach chair moved down here on the beach, away from the hotel and the few people around the pool.

She took her dark glasses off, massaged the bridge of her nose and looked out at the water. A man was jogging on the beach, not a good fast jog, more of a slow-paced trot. No wonder, she thought. It was too hot even for that. As she watched, he started past, then saw her and stopped only a few feet away.

"*Buenos días,*" he said cheerfully.

Kristen hesitated before she said, "Good morning."

"Ah, you're an American. I thought because of your fair hair you might be Scandinavian."

"No." She looked down at the financial report, because she had no intention of carrying on a conversation with this Spanish... The word *dude* came to mind. That almost brought a grin. She suppressed it and tried for a frown.

He moved closer and stood in front of her, muscled legs firmly planted in the sand, tall and tanned and barefoot, wearing faded cutoffs. A beach bum, she decided, and she would certainly have found him attractive, if—and the *if* was a big one—this were her year for beach-type Spanish dudes.

"You are staying at the hotel, yes?"

Kristen nodded.

"You look very warm. Wouldn't you like to swim?"

She looked out at the emerald-green water of the Mediterranean. For maybe three and a half seconds, she was tempted. Then the temptation passed. She rustled the papers she was holding and said, "I have work to do."

"And I am interrupting you." He smiled, his teeth very white in his tanned face, and in a friendly, cajoling voice said, "You should enjoy. Swim a little, drink some wine."

She looked up at him, looked into eyes as green as the Med, and for a moment, though she could not have explained why—perhaps because of the sun—she felt strangely disoriented. Then, because she did, and because she didn't know how else to get rid of him, she said, "I have to go in now." And, standing, she gathered up the papers she had been working on.

Still smiling, he followed her movements with his gaze and looked at her, all of her that was so plainly visible in her skimpy blue bikini. Turning back to the beach chair, she picked up her white terry-cloth beach coat, slipped it over her shoulders—and dropped her book.

He bent quickly to pick it up. *"Business Management in the Nineties,"* he read aloud. Then, with a smile, he said, "But you are in Spain, *señorita.* You should be reading of love and romance, not business."

Kristen snatched the book out of his hand. Her fingers brushed his, and she pulled back as though she'd been burned. He looked at her strangely and stepped back a pace. Still smiling, he said, "Until *mañana, señorita,"* and turning he jogged away.

She put her sunglasses back on and watched him. A dude, she thought, remembering Tillie's words. And, with a nudge of regret, she left the beach to go back to the hotel.

Kristen saw him again the following morning. He waved, but he didn't stop. And that, she tried to tell herself, was just fine with her.

That afternoon, when the last rays of the sun sparkled golden on the waves and the sky turned from bright flamingo to mauve, she saw him from her balcony. He was running fast this time, long legs striding out, arms pumping. Instead of the ragged cutoffs, he wore French-cut swim trunks. His body was well muscled and lean, his skin turned the color of bronze in the last sun rays of the fading day.

He stopped a few yards from the hotel before he sprinted across the beach and into the sea. He swam straight out, diving beneath the rolling waves, his strokes strong and smooth. He swam for a long time, and when at last he came out of the water he stood, legs apart, to sluice the water off his body and run his hands through his dark hair. Suddenly, almost as though he were aware of her watching him, he looked up toward the hotel. And saw her, she thought, standing there on her balcony.

For a long moment, they simply stared at each other. Then Kristen stepped back into her room.

That night, though she took two sleeping pills instead of one, sleep was a long time coming. When it did, she dreamed of the tall, dark beachcomber. He came toward her and, taking her hand, pulled her out of the beach chair and said, "Come, we will swim."

But when they waded into the water, it turned to icy-cold slush, and she was back in New York again, at work again, wearing one of her dark tailored suits, her blond hair pulled off her face in a tight chignon.

The meeting was about to start. She couldn't find her notes. Had to find them. Couldn't go to the meeting without them. The phone rang. The intercom buzzed. Her two secretaries ran in, followed by the chief chemist and the head of production.

"Hurry, hurry, hurry!" they all cried.

Get the reports! Pick up the phone! Answer your intercom!

She woke with a start, sitting straight up in bed, heart beating hard, perspiration beading her body. She took deep breaths and told herself to relax. She tried to listen to the sound of the waves coming in through the open French doors, but the sharp, shrill ring of the phone and the buzz of the intercom still echoed in her ears. And Dr. Alexander's voice: "You're headed for a breakdown. You have to get away."

This, whatever *this* was, had probably been building for a long time. It had come to a head that cold March morning a week ago. She'd washed her hair before she discovered her hair dryer wouldn't work. She'd towel-dried her hair, rolled it into a damp bun and quickly dressed.

The limousine, with Artie at the wheel, was waiting for her when she hurried out of her apartment. He drove her to the office. Yesterday's snow had turned to slush, and the streets of New York looked gray and dirty. When Artie stopped in front of the office building, she thanked him and said, "I'm going to work late tonight. I'll call you when I know what time I'll be through."

She stepped out of the limo, and just as she reached the curb a taxi careered around the corner and threw gray and muddy slush all over her new suede coat.

She was still muttering under her breath when she went into her office. Tillie, big dark-rimmed glasses down over her nose, curly red hair loose about her pixie's face, greeted her with a cup of black coffee and the words "You're late, Kris. The meeting is about to— My God! What happened to your coat?"

"Don't ask." Kristen accepted the coffee, took a gulp, and reached for the agenda.

"Guess you have to deal with the Marilyn thing," Tillie said. "I know that'll be difficult, Kris."

The Marilyn thing. Meaning Marilyn Evans, a friend from her college days, a woman she had brought into the company and trained. Marilyn, who had been selling New Woman Cosmetics formulas to a rival cosmetics firm.

Tillie was the one who had first suspected Marilyn, and though Kristen had been reluctant to believe it, she'd done some investigating and found it was true. Two days ago, she had confronted Marilyn about her duplicity in selling New Woman's secrets.

"You're through here," she'd said.

"It's because of Ben, isn't it? You're doing this because of him, not because of the company."

"Ben?" She'd looked at Marilyn, too shocked to say anything. What in the world did Ben have to do with this?

She and Ben Livingston had been dating for the past two years. They'd talked of marriage, but for one reason or another they'd kept putting it off. When she mentioned it, he hadn't been ready. Six months later, when he brought it up, she'd been the one who was uncertain, especially when he'd brought up the subject of children. He wanted them, she didn't.

But when Marilyn said, "It's because of Ben, isn't it? Because it's me he wants, not you." Kristen had been totally flabbergasted. Marilyn had laughed, a low throaty chuckle. "Hell, Kristen," she'd said, "you couldn't keep a boyfriend in college. What made you think you could keep a man like Ben?"

She told herself when she started into the board meeting that day that her decision to fire Marilyn had nothing to do with Ben. She would not allow the hurt and betrayal she felt to influence her decision. And it didn't. As CEO, she handled the matter of Marilyn quickly and efficiently. When George Terhune, her vice president in charge of sales, said maybe they should give Marilyn another chance, Ed Marcus, her executive vice president, said, "To hell with that. She should be prosecuted."

"No," Kristen said. "Prosecution would involve a scandal. We don't need that."

When at last the meeting adjourned, she went back to her office.

"You handled that like a pro," Tillie, who had been at the meeting, told her. She poured a cup of coffee and handed it to Kristen. When Kristen picked it up, her hands started to shake. She spilled the coffee, saw Tillie's startled face, and then, for a reason she wasn't sure she understood even now, she started to cry.

She couldn't stop. Tillie took her home. When, after an hour, she still couldn't stop crying, Tillie called Dr. Alexander. He came to the house, gave her some kind of injection and ordered her to bed. Three days later, when she wanted to go back to work, he said, "Absolutely not. I'm ordering you to take a month off."

Tillie had spent her two-week vacation in Spain last year. "At this absolutely great hotel," she said. "Believe me, Kris, you'll love it."

So Kristen had come to Spain, here to Santa Cruz de la Palma, on the Costa del Sol. But only for a week. She would take the sleeping pills Dr. Alexander had given her. She would rest and swim and try to sleep.

She looked at the bedside clock. Two-thirty. And because she knew sleep would be a long time coming, she turned on the bedside lamp and picked up the financial reports. New Woman Cosmetics was her baby, and even though she was some four thousand miles away, she was still in charge.

* * *

The following day, Señor Zavala, the owner of the hotel, invited her to lunch on the hotel patio overlooking the sea. A short, pleasantly chubby man in his early fifties, he seemed the personification of a Spanish gentleman.

He held her chair and, when she was seated, told her he had taken the liberty of ordering white wine and suggested the gazpacho and a seafood salad.

Kristen smiled and, with a nod, said, *"Gracias. That sounds wonderful."*

He asked her if this was her first visit to Spain, and when she told him it was, he said, "There is much to see here on the Costa del Sol. I hope you will stay long enough to visit some of the charming towns nearby."

"I know my reservation was for a month," Kristen said, "but I'm afraid I won't be able to stay that long." She took another sip of her wine, and when she put her glass down she looked up and saw the tall, tanned beachcomber coming across the patio in their direction.

"Don Ramon," he said. *"¿Cómo estás?* It's nice to see you." He looked at Kristen, bowed and added, *"Señorita."*

"Sit down, sit down." Señor Zavala motioned him to a chair. "You're just in time to join us for lunch, Fernando."

"I don't want to intrude."

"Intrude? No, no, my friend. I insist you join us." And to Kristen he said, "Allow me to introduce my friend, Fernando Ibarra. He has a house a little farther down on the beach. Fernando, this is Miss Kristen Fielding from New York. She is to be our guest for a while." He smiled at Kristen. "You must not be in a hurry to return to New York. You must stay with us for the month you had planned, yes?"

Fernando Ibarra offered his hand. She gave him her standard business handshake. *"Señorita,"* he said with an odd little smile.

He was wearing jeans and a blue-and-white striped T-shirt. And he was still barefoot.

He was, she reluctantly admitted to herself, one of the best-looking, most masculine-looking, men she'd ever met. His features were classic, his green eyes fringed with eyelashes that most women would have given their teeth for. His short, slightly curly hair, was a Spanish black. He was tall, six-one or six-two, and there wasn't an ounce of fat on his broad-shouldered body. His accent was charming, and very likely he was, too. A charming beachcomber. Uh-uh, she thought. He definitely wasn't her type.

"Fernando is an attorney." Señor Zavala signaled to the waiter for another glass and, when he had filled Ibarra's glass, said, "But you are not working now, my friend?"

"Like Señorita Fielding, I, too, am taking a short vacation."

"You are always taking a short vacation." Zavala laughed and, to Kristen, said, "Fernando knows how to live, *señorita*. When he works, I am told by business friends in Málaga, he is the best lawyer on the Costa del Sol. And when he plays . . ." Zavala leaned back in his chair and rolled his eyes.

"I travel, Don Ramon," Ibarra said. "But that, too, is business."

"*Sí, sí,* I know. I also know you enjoy the good life."

"But that is what life is for, yes?" Fernando Ibarra smiled at Kristen. "For if we do not enjoy life, then what is the reason for living?"

She bristled, even as she wondered why she suddenly felt so defensive.

"Have you visited other places in Spain?" Ibarra asked.

Kristen shook her head. "I flew into Málaga and came directly here."

"I asked her the very same question," Don Ramon said. "I told her that she must see something besides the hotel and the beach. At least some of the charming towns that are not too far from here." He drained his glass of wine, wiped his mouth with his white linen napkin and said, "You will take her, Fernando. Show her Mijas and Nerja."

"It would be my pleasure, Don Ramon." He smiled at Kristen. "Will tomorrow be convenient, Señorita Fielding?"

She tried to think of an excuse. She had to work. She planned to spend the day at the beach. She was expecting a fax.

"Shall we say at nine?" he asked, before she could think of anything. "Here in front of the hotel?"

"It's kind of you to offer," she said. "But really, I don't want to put you out."

"Put me out? I'm sorry. I do not know that expression."

"To trouble you," she said.

"I assure you, Señorita, it would be my pleasure, not my trouble." He smiled. "Nine o'clock, *sí?*"

She told herself that of course she couldn't go traipsing around the countryside with this man, who, although he was a friend of Señor Zavala's, was a stranger to her. She would tell him she had to work, tell him—

"*Bien,*" Señor Zavala said. "Fernando will show you some of our beautiful coast. You will have lunch, drink some wine, and perhaps after all you will decide to stay for a month."

She looked at him, then at Fernando Ibarra.

"Nine?" Ibarra asked, his green eyes intent on hers.

And, though she did not intend to, Kristen found herself saying, "Yes. At nine."

"*Hecho.* Done." Señor Zavala signaled to the waiter to bring another bottle of wine, and when it was opened and their glasses had been filled, he raised his glass and said, "To Spain, to the lovely Señorita Fielding, and to the wonderful day she and Fernando will have tomorrow."

He touched his glass to Kristen's, then to Fernando's, and with a smile added, "And we will convince her to stay longer than a few days, *sí?*"

Fernando looked at her over their raised glasses. "*Sí,*" he said. "We will convince her."

Chapter Two

Kristen was waiting for Fernando when he pulled up in front of the hotel, and he smiled to himself, because she looked so unlike the other foreign visitors who came to southern Spain—the Americans in their too-bright shirts and shorts, the tall Scandinavian women who sunned topless, and the chic French women who did the same.

Kristen Fielding's white silk blouse was buttoned at the throat. With it she wore a dark blue skirt that came several inches below her knees, and espadrilles that laced around her ankles. She wore her hair pulled back off her face in a rather severe manner, and her only makeup was a touch of pale lipstick. The total effect, he thought, was one of planned plainness. But it didn't work, for no matter how she might have tried to diminish it, her beauty shone through. She was tall and blond, an ice maiden from New York City, somehow out of place here in the warmth of sunny Spain.

"Have you had breakfast?" he asked when he opened the door to let her in. "Would you like to stop someplace for coffee?"

"No, thank you."

He hurried around to his side of the car and, when he wheeled out of the hotel driveway, said, "You don't mind that the top is down?"

Kristen shook her head. "I have a scarf in my purse." She opened her bag, took out a blue-and-white scarf and tied it over her hair.

"I thought we'd go to Mijas this morning. It's not too far."

"Wherever you think," Kristen said. "I don't want to keep you away from whatever you might have to do."

He laughed—it was a good, rich sound—and said, "My dear Señorita Fielding, all I have to do on a morning like this is enjoy it. Like you, I, too, am on vacation. It's a beautiful day, the sun is warm, the air smells of springtime and I'm with a beautiful woman. What more could a man ask for?"

She ignored the "beautiful woman" part and said, "Yes, it is a beautiful day, and it was nice of Señor Zavala to suggest I see more of the countryside. But I'm afraid he trapped you into taking me."

"Nonsense. He would have taken you himself, but he is married and his wife wouldn't like it."

"Are you married, Señor Ibarra?"

"No, *señorita,* I'm not. And I would like it very much if you would call me Fernando. May I call you Kristen?"

He pronounced it "Krees-teen," and she said, "Tin. It's pronounced Kris-*tin*."

"*Muy bien*. Kris*tin*. But it is like Christine, yes?"

"More or less," she said.

There was very little conversation after that. She leaned back in the seat and began to enjoy the countryside, for after all, he was right, the day was beautiful, the sun was warm, and as long as she was here she might as well enjoy herself.

It had been dark when she flew into Málaga, and all she'd seen of Spain so far was the airport in that city and the hotel where she was staying. She liked the beach, of course, but it was nice to see some of the countryside. And this countryside was beautiful indeed. The fields that stretched for as far as she could see were golden in the sun. Fat, languid sheep, guarded by ever-vigilant dogs, nibbled on meadow grass while shepherds, old men with sunburned faces, their heads protected by the Spanish beret, called out to their dogs in guttural voices.

They drove past groves of olive trees, through whitewashed villages, and other villages the very color of the earth from which they seemed to have sprung. There were gardens filled with roses and geraniums, vine arbors and shaded bowers. And in the distance the crumbled but still stately remnants of Moorish castles.

Castles in Spain, Kristen thought. And, though not quite at ease with Fernando Ibarra, she was glad now that she had accepted his invitation.

She wasn't sure how much time had gone by when he said, "There ahead, that is Mijas." And she saw on the rise of a mountain a town that was little more than a village, with a cluster of houses so white that in the morning sun they were almost blinding.

"It looks..." She hesitated, unable to describe the impact of this place that seemed carved out of the mountains. "I don't know, like something out of the *Arabian Nights.*"

"Moorish," Fernando said. "The Moors occupied the kingdom of what they called al-Andalus for almost eight hundred years. You see their influence all over Spain, but particularly here in the south. The great mosque of Córdoba, the Giralda minaret in Sevilla and the wonderful Alcazaba Palace in Granada were all the work of Moorish architects and craftsmen."

He slowed the car and turned to Kristen. "There is so much to see here," he said. "It would be my pleasure to show all of these places to you—Sevilla, Ronda, Córdoba, and of course you should see Granada, the gardens of the Alhambra there, and the Gypsy caves of Sacromonte." He smiled. "Please, Señorita Kristen, you must allow me to show you my Spain."

"I don't know," she said. "I have a job—"

"What do you do?"

"I'm the president and CEO of a cosmetics company in New York."

"*Pues,* if you are the head of the company, then you can give yourself a vacation."

"*Pues,*" she said. "I don't think so."

"You speak Spanish." He looked surprised. "I didn't know that."

"I studied it in college, and lately, I've been taking a few night classes."

"You work too hard, I think."

And you, she wanted to say, don't seem to work at all. That bothered her, for though it was obvious he wasn't the beach bum she had first thought him to be, he seemed to have all the free time in the world. She wasn't used to that kind of man. The men she dated were, like Ben, driven to succeed in whatever profession they were in. They rarely took time for a leisurely drive like this. When they dined out, whether for lunch or dinner, it was usually for business. Deals were made over a second martini or on the ninth hole of a swank golf course.

Fernando was different. He acted as though he had all the time in the world to simply enjoy life.

They wound their way up and around the mountain until at last they reached the small main square of Mijas.

"We'll leave the car here," Fernando said. "Most of the streets are too narrow to drive in. It is better to walk."

She took her scarf off. Though she had covered her hair, tendrils of it had come loose about her face and at the back of her neck to give her a softer, more feminine look. A look he most definitely liked.

"Come," he said when he took her hand to help her out of the car. "Let's go exploring."

Up and down narrow cobbled streets they went, past whitewashed houses with red-tiled roofs and balconies that spilled all manner of flowers from earthen pots. It was a charming town, a centuries-old town.

Fernando took her to the chapel of Mijas's patroness, the Virgen de la Pena, and to the bullring. In a tiny shop on one of the cobbled streets she bought a postcard to send to Tillie, and when her back was turned Fernando bought her a white T-shirt with the words Mijas Is for Lovers emblazoned in red.

"A present," he said, and laughed when she made a face.

Then, while Kristen watched, he bought six children's T-shirts in different colors. She raised her eyebrows. He'd told her he wasn't married. Had he lied? Did he have a wife and children he left at home when he went on these little jaunts with foreign tourists.

He turned and saw her watching him. "Presents," he said with a smile. "Children love presents."

Whose children? she wanted to ask, but didn't.

It was almost noon when they left the shop. The tour buses were filling up the square and spewing exhaust fumes into the air. "The town is too busy with tourists now," Fernando said. "If you've seen enough, we'll go on to Marbella for lunch."

"I've seen enough," Kristen answered. "But, really—"

"*Pero realmente*. Is that what you were going to say? That *realmente* I don't have to take you to lunch? That *realmente* we should go back to the hotel?" He reached for her hand. "Believe me, Señorita Kristen, I'm enjoying the day. I wish you would, too."

"I am," she said, and knew that it was true, for after all, she *was* enjoying herself. Well, except for that small nudge of suspicion that maybe, in spite of telling her he wasn't, he really was married.

Once in the car, she relaxed enough to forget about putting the scarf on. The wind felt good, and when the chignon began to sag she took the hairpins out and let her hair blow free.

And because the sun was hot, she even opened the first two buttons of her blouse. With a contented sigh, she leaned back against the seat, and didn't notice that the wind ruffled her blouse just enough that a wisp of lacy bra was visible.

Fernando glanced at her and smiled. And though he made no comment, he thought that perhaps there was hope for this very attractive *gringa* after all.

He took her to a restaurant on the beach, where they sat on the patio under a striped umbrella facing the sea. He ordered a pitcher of sangria, and when it was served he touched his glass to hers and said, "Welcome to Spain, Señorita Kristen." And, because he wanted to know, asked, "You are not married?"

"No, Señor Ibarra, I'm not." She hesitated. "Are you?"

He looked surprised by her question. "Of course not," he said. "I have already told you, yes? Do you think I would be with you like this if I were married?"

She blushed and looked down at her glass.

"Have you ever been married?"

Kristen shook her head and took a sip of the sangria. It was cold and delicious. "No," she said. "I haven't had time for marriage."

Time? he wondered. He wanted to ask if there was someone special in her life, and knew it was too soon for such a personal question. Too soon, too, for personal confidences. Instead, he asked about New York, about the plays she had seen, the concerts she might have gone to.

"I was there last year. It's a wonderfully exciting city, isn't it? I saw a play every night and tasted food I had never had tasted before. Your Carnegie Delicatessen. *Dios mío...* " He closed his eyes and sighed. "Such sandwiches," he said. *"Que divino."*

That made her laugh, and the sound of it, there on that sunlit patio, made him want to reach out and touch her. But he didn't. Instead, he said, "What would you like to eat? The seafood here is excellent."

"You choose," she said, still smiling.

"*Langostino*, cold lobster, and a green salad, I think. And perhaps to begin we will have some *gambas*, crawfish, and *bocarones*, small fish prepared in vinaigrette. Is that all right?"

"It sounds wonderful," Kristen said. And it was. The *bocarones*, eaten with hard, crusty bread, were delicious. So were the crawfish. They finished one pitcher of sangria, and he asked for another to drink with the cold lobster.

They talked more easily now, and once, when he said something funny and she laughed, he reached for her hand and said, "I love to hear you laugh. You should do it more often."

And when he didn't let go of her hand, she found herself looking at him, really looking at him, into eyes as green as the sea, at a full and sensuous mouth that seemed to have been molded for kissing. She felt a ping of something not at all unpleasant, and when he brushed his thumb over the back of her hand she felt a quickening of her breath, a sudden warmth.

"I want to see you again," he said. "Tonight and tomorrow and the day after that and the day after that. You must stay, at least long enough to let me show you this part of Spain."

"Señor Ibarra... Fernando..." She remembered the six children's T-shirts and tried to pull her hand away. But he held on to it for a moment more.

"Tonight we will go to Torremolinos, yes? There is a place where we can have a wonderful steak and drink red Rioja wine."

Maybe he'd bought the shirts for the children of friends. Maybe they were for nieces and nephews. She pulled her hand away. "I came to Spain to rest," she said, "not to..." She shook her head, not sure how to tell him she hadn't come to have a romantic fling, that she really was not at all this spontaneous and that she never relaxed this way with strangers, certainly not on a first date, if indeed this was a date. And not with a man who might have a wife and six children tucked somewhere out of sight.

"Afterward, we will dance," he said. "There is a small place right on the beach. You will like it, I promise you will."

She shook her head and tried to look severe. "I came to Spain to rest," she said. "Not to—"

"Not to what?" he asked with a smile. And before she could answer he said, "The *espuma de chocolate*—the chocolate mousse, yes?—is very good here. We will have some. And coffee. Good Spanish coffee."

He spoke of other things then, of the University of Salamanca, where he had studied for his law degree, of Paris, which he said was for him one of the most beautiful cities in the world—next to Madrid of course.

He told her about his friendship with Ramon Zavala. "His wife, Maria Luisa, is charming," he said.

"They have nine children and all of them, *gracias a Dios,* look like Maria Luisa."

"Nine children?" Kristen made a face. "Good Lord, why?"

He looked surprised. Shocked. "You don't like children?"

She shrugged. "They're all right. I suppose. But nine?" She shook her head. "Good Lord," she said again.

He had little to say after that. He looked a bit grim, she thought, but once they were in the car he seemed to relax. He drove for a way along the waterfront. Now, in the late afternoon, fishermen were coming in with their day's catch, bringing their boats in to shore, spreading nets on the beach to dry. There were bonfires on the sand, and women were roasting some of the freshly caught fish on long sticks to sell to passersby.

The air was filled with the sharp tang of the sea, fresh fish and smoke, and Kristen was glad to be here, driving along the coast with Fernando Ibarra, feeling the wind in her hair, the sun on her face.

When they were back on the highway again, he said, "It's been a long day. You must have a siesta before we go out for dinner."

Dinner? She didn't think so.

It was almost five when he pulled into the driveway of her hotel. He came around to her side of the car to help her out and, holding her hand, said, "I will pick you up at eight, yes?"

"Fernando, really, I—"

"Do not say no," he said. And, taking her hand, he brought it to his lips.

She felt the brush of his kiss against her skin. Still holding her hand, he looked into her eyes and said, "Eight. Yes?"

She took a quivering breath and, though she had told herself she would not, said, "Yes."

"Good!" He squeezed her hand. "Until tonight then, *mi muñaquita.*"

Muñaquita? She was in her room before she remembered what the word meant. *Doll. My little doll.*

"Not hardly!" she said aloud. But then she looked in the mirror and discovered she was smiling.

She wore one of the dresses Tillie had insisted she buy for the trip. It was black, and short, with thin straps over the shoulder and what she thought of as a too-daring décolletage. With it she wore high-heeled sandals. Her hair, as always, was pulled back into a chignon, and in her ears she wore pearl drop earrings.

Though she had told herself that she would not nap, that she *never* napped, that she would only lie down for a few minutes, it was almost seven when she awakened. The room was bathed in the soft glow of twilight and she could smell the sea. She lay there for a moment, not sure why she was smiling, then got up, took a leisurely bath—a luxury she rarely took time for in New York—and dressed.

Fernando was talking to Ramon Zavala when she came into the lobby. He looked very elegant, very handsome in dark trousers and a white dinner jacket.

Señor Zavala said, "Ah, there you are, Señorita Fielding. Did you have a nice day?" And before she could answer, he went on, "Yes, of course you did. Your cheeks are sunburned and you look quite beautiful.'' He gave an exaggerated sigh. ''You almost make a man wish he did not have nine children.'' He winked at Fernando. ''Soon to be ten.''

Fernando took her hand and, to Ramon, said, ''Shame on you, the father of nine and a half children, for flirting with my lady.''

''Flirting?'' Ramon Zavala's eyes widened in mock horror. ''This was not flirting, my friend, merely intense appreciation.''

With a laugh, Fernando took Kristen's hand and said, ''Let me take you away from this terrible man with the roving eye.'' He waved a farewell to Ramon and led Kristen out to his car.

The top was up. ''So your hair will not blow,'' he said.

And she said, ''I can't believe he has nine children and wants more.''

''But Maria Luisa and Ramon love children,'' Fernando said, as though surprised that she would find ten too many. ''He has money enough to support his family and educate his children.'' And he asked her again, as he had earlier, ''Don't you like children?''

''Of course I do.'' Her mouth tightened. ''Doesn't everybody?''

Fernando mumbled an indistinct reply and looked straight ahead.

Torremolinos, when they arrived, was awash with people: jeans-clad teenagers of all nationalities, some with backpacks, a few of them drunk, most of them boisterous, shopkeepers, bank employees, dark-eyed secretaries in short skirts, well-dressed Spanish gentlemen and their ladies and well-heeled tourists.

"First a *tapa* bar," Fernando said. Taking Kristen's arm, he led her into a corner stand-up bar, where he ordered shrimp, cheese and two glasses of red wine. The place was filled with both tourists and locals. A dark-skinned man wearing a full-sleeved white shirt with a red vest sat on a three-legged stool in one corner of the room, strumming a guitar.

"In a bad imitation of flamenco," Fernando said as he took a bite of shrimp. "When we go to Granada, I will take you to Sacromonte, where you will hear the Gypsies play real flamenco. As long as you are here, you should stay and enjoy." He held a *gamba* to her lips. "Taste," he said. "It is good, yes?"

There was something intimate and, yes, sensual in taking the food from his fingers. A bit of the sauce stayed on the corner of her lip, and before she could wipe it off he touched it and, instead of wiping it on one of the small napkins, brought his finger to his mouth and, with his eyes on hers, licked it off.

"Delicious," he murmured.

She felt a sudden spark of fire curl in her body, and quickly looked away.

The restaurant he took her to was beautifully elegant. He ordered a bottle of red Rioja and two steaks. "Medium rare?" he asked.

The steaks were good, and so was the wine. She rarely drank more than one glass, and that only at an occasional business luncheon or dinner. It had always been important to her that she remain clearheaded and in control, especially when it came to business. Even with Ben, she had never had more than one glass of white wine.

This afternoon she'd had more than her share of sangria, and now here she was, sipping what was probably her third glass of this wonderful hearty red wine, feeling good—not tipsy, just good. And, after all, Fernando Ibarra was nice. No, more than nice. Charming and thoughtful, and so good-looking that all the women in the restaurant stared at him when they first entered. Even now, they cast surreptitious glances his way. Two of them, with their dates in tow, had stopped by the table to say, "Fernando! How nice to see you. We must get together soon."

Both times he'd stood, shaken hands with their escorts, and introduced Kristen. That made her think that after all perhaps he wasn't married.

After dinner, he took her to a café on the beach. He ordered cognac, and when the music changed from disco to slow he took her hand and led her out onto the dance floor.

He was a good dancer. He curled his fingers around hers and brought her hand up to rest against his chest. A rumba segued into a bolero. He urged her closer, his hand warm against her back, as they moved to the pulsing Latin rhythm.

The music stopped, but still he stood, holding her hand cupped in his against his chest. "You feel good in my arms," he said. "I like dancing with you."

She tried to look away, tried to think of something clever to say, and couldn't. Instead, she only stood there, looking up at him. And when he said, "It's too warm in here. Would you like a walk on the beach?" she nodded.

When they left the café, he put her arm through his, and together they strolled down the few steps to the beach. She removed her shoes, and he took them from her.

It was cooler near the water, and he asked, "Are you cold?" and when she said, "A little," he took off his white jacket and draped it over her shoulders.

"Is that better?" And then, because it was something he had wanted to do the very first time he saw her, he closed his hands around the lapels of the white jacket and, drawing her close, he kissed her.

She stood still, not answering his kiss, but not moving away.

He murmured, "Kristen..." He brought her closer and, though she stiffened, he held her that way. And kissed her again, slowly, gently, until at last her lips parted and softened. Even then, his kiss was gentle.

When at last he let her go, he said, "If I have offended you, I am sorry, but I've wanted to do that all day." He stroked a tendril of hair back from her face. "It was worth waiting for." He smiled. "I fear it could be habit-forming."

"Fernando, I—"

"Shh..." he whispered, and stopped her words with another kiss. A kiss that, while still gentle, became more intense, more thrilling, than any kiss had ever been for her.

She clung to him, holding him as he held her, even as she told herself she should not be like this. She didn't know him. She'd be in Spain for only another few days. She didn't want to do this, to start something.

She stepped away. "Don't," she said. "I don't want..." She took a deep breath to steady herself. "I'm not a casual person," she said.

"I didn't think you were."

"I mean, I don't believe in vacation romances."

"Neither do I." He cupped her face. "I don't think that is what this is, Kristen. Perhaps I don't know what it is yet, but I do not think it is only a vacation romance."

He took her hand and brought it to his lips. "Now I will take you safely back to your hotel. We will put the top down, and perhaps the wind will cool our hungry hearts."

Our hungry hearts. She felt hot tears sting her eyes, and looked away. But she let him take her hand, and when they reached the car and he put the top down and pulled her closer, she let her head rest against his shoulder.

And, though she did not think she would, she slept all the way back to Santa Cruz de la Palma.

Chapter Three

Kristen saw Fernando the following day, the day after that, and the day after that. And though she had told herself she should make plans to leave, she didn't.

Each morning Fernando joined her on the beach for a swim. In a French-cut bikini, he was something to see; his shoulders and chest were broad and finely muscled, his stomach was flat, his hips were narrow. His long legs were strong and his skin was tanned to a fine honey-bronze.

The first morning they went in the water together he said, "Why would you not swim with me the first time I asked you?"

"I didn't know you, and..." She blushed and shook her head.

"And what?"

"I was embarrassed. I'm used to a one-piece suit, and there was almost nothing to the bikini my friend bought for me."

"Embarrassed? *Pero, por Dios,* Kristen, you have a beautiful body."

"I'm too thin."

"Not in the places where it counts," he said with a grin. For, while it was true she needed a bit of fattening up, she really was a trim package of a woman. Her breasts, though small, were high and firm, her long legs were beautifully shaped, and he could span her waist, if she ever let him get that close, with his two hands.

He liked looking at her, whether in a bikini, the black dress she'd worn that first night, or a high-necked blouse. There was something about her, a grace of movement, a ladylike delicacy, that pleased him. He even liked her cool reserve, because to him it was a challenge to break through that reserve, to find the warmth of the woman beneath.

She became more relaxed when they were swimming, for it was as if the water somehow released her. She was a good swimmer, and it was obvious she took great pleasure in the water. On the third morning they swam together, a wave brought them closer, so close that he felt the length of her salt-slick body against his. It was all he could do not to put his arms around her. He wanted to kiss her until they both went a little crazy. Wanted to carry her to a shady and secluded section of the beach and make love with her.

But he hesitated. She had responded to his kisses the other night, but only for a moment before backing away. Perhaps for her those few kisses had been enough, but for him they had only been a sample, a tantalizing taste of pleasures yet to come.

Another wave brought them closer, and this time he could not hold back. He cupped her face. "Kristen," he murmured, and kissed her.

She made as though to pull back, but he held her and kissed her until her lips parted under his. They treaded water, bodies close, legs entangled. He felt the cool softness of her breasts against his chest, and because he could not help himself, because he had wanted to touch her this way since the day he had first seen her, he cupped her breast.

"No," she said against his lips. But instead of letting her go, he eased the scanty top down and sucked his breath in at the sight of her. He touched her gently, reverently. Her skin was like velvet, and though she made as if to pull away, she did not. The kiss deepened as he caressed her. She moaned softly, and the sound of it, that soft sound of passion, tightened his body with a terrible need.

"Kristen," he said, just as a wave, higher than the others, crashed over their heads. They came up sputtering and apart. She pulled her top up and said, "We—we'd better go in."

"You go ahead." His face looked strained with tension. "I think I'll swim a few more minutes."

But almost fifteen minutes went by before he came in to shore. And that night, when he took her back to the hotel after dinner in Torremolinos, he offered no more than a quick good-night kiss.

The next morning, after their swim, he walked her back to the patio of her hotel. "I have to take care of

things at home," he said. "I'll see you later this afternoon."

He kissed her cheek and, with a smile, turned and
walked away from her. She wasn't sure how she felt
about that. A little relieved, a little disappointed. A
little curious.

She told Tillie about him one morning when she
called the office.

Tillie asked how she was enjoying the hotel and if
she had seen anything at all of Andalusia.

"I've been to Mijas," she said. "And to Torremolinos for dinner."

"Alone?" Tillie asked.

"No."

"With Señor Zavala and his wife? Or dare I ask if
you've met someone?"

"You can ask." Kristen let the three words hang in
the air a moment or two, then, with a smile in her
voice, said, "His name is Fernando Ibarra, and yes,
Til, he's tall, dark and handsome."

"And Spanish." Tillie laughed. "God, Kris, I'm so
glad. Do you like him? What does he do for a living?
Is he single? How old is he?"

"Yes, I like him. He's a lawyer. He's single." She
hesitated. "Yes, I'm sure he's single. I—I guess he's
thirty-five or thirty-six."

"Well?"

"Well, what?"

"Have you—? You know."

"Til! Shame on you. Of course not."

"Why not?"

Kristen's indignation faded, and she laughed. "Because I don't believe in holiday romances."

"Maybe it could be more than that. You could always commute."

"Between New York and Spain? Sure."

"Then maybe you should enjoy what you can, while you can."

"I don't think so. How are things at the office?"

"I hate to tell you, but we're doing just fine. Stay in Spain as long as you want to." Tillie hesitated. "Ben has been calling. He wanted to know where you were. I only told him you were in Europe, but if you want me to I'll tell him where."

"Yes, do that. If he calls again, tell him I'm in Timbuktu."

"Attagirl."

After Kristen hung up, she smiled. She'd really meant it when she told Tillie to tell Ben she was in Timbuktu. The pain of his betrayal had ebbed; she no longer cared what he did or with whom.

She and Fernando were more at ease with each other now. Actually, she was more at ease with herself. She no longer felt uncomfortable in the bikini or in the short dresses Tillie had chosen for her. As for the chignon, it had disappeared. Now she wore her hair in a ponytail, or loose about her shoulders. Because Fernando said he liked it that way.

One morning, to please him, she wore the red Mijas Is For Lovers T-shirt over her bikini. He laughed when he saw it, and said, "*¡Andale!* Let's go back to Mijas!"

She told herself she would enjoy her time with Fernando, and when she had to return to New York she would be able to give him a goodbye kiss with no regrets. Perhaps she'd return to Spain next year; perhaps he would visit her in New York. In the meantime, she would relax and enjoy both Fernando and Spain.

One afternoon they drove to Ronda, one of the oldest towns in Spain, he told her, reached by what Kristen thought was probably the most spectacular mountain road in this part of Spain.

The top was down on the convertible, and the sun was warm on their faces. Fernando played romantic Spanish songs on the tape deck and sang along with them in a rich baritone. Now and then he reached for her hand and, with a smile, said, "When I am happy, I sing. Today I am happy."

When at last they reached Ronda, he parked in the shade of a giant tree and said, "Ronda is small, but interesting. Come, I will show it to you."

They drank wine at an outside table overlooking El Tajo, a deep ravine that was a breathtaking nine hundred feet across. It was on his second glass of wine that Fernando finally asked the question he had wanted to ask since the day he had met her.

"Is there someone in your life?" he said. "Someone you are serious about?"

"No." Kristen looked at him across the table. "There was, but there isn't anymore."

"May I ask why?"

"He betrayed me with a woman I thought was my friend."

Fernando's dark brows drew together in a frown and, reaching for her hand, he said, "That must have hurt you."

"Yes," she said with open frankness. "It did. But it doesn't anymore."

"I'm glad."

And because he had asked, she could ask. "What about you, Fernando? Is there someone special in your life?"

"There are many people in my life who are special to me. But a woman? No, there is no woman in my life."

"But there has been," she said with a certainty.

"Of course." He laughed. "But no one with whom I have wanted to spend my life." He seemed on the verge of saying more, but he didn't. They finished their wine and, after they had strolled around the town, he said, "The mountain road is treacherous at night. We'd better start back to Santa Cruz."

He drove at a leisurely pace, and when they pulled into the driveway of the hotel he said, "I have plans tonight, but I would like it very much if you would have dinner with me tomorrow night."

Did he have another date? He'd spent so much time with her that she was pretty sure by now that he wasn't married. He had told her there was no one special in his life, but that didn't mean he wasn't seeing someone else. That was no concern of hers, of course. But still, she wondered.

"Tomorrow night?" he asked.

"Yes, all right."

"At my home. I will come for you at seven-thirty, if that's all right."

His home? That gave her pause, but she said, "Yes, Fernando, seven-thirty is fine."

He brought her hand to his lips and kissed it. "Until then," he said. And he waited until she went in before he returned to the car and drove away.

His expression was thoughtful as he headed back down the road. Was it too soon to have invited her to his home? Should he have waited until their relationship formed a more solid foundation? But there was so little time, for soon Kristen would leave to return to New York. He wanted her in the intimacy of home. He would tell her then. Yes, tomorrow night he would tell her.

She wasn't sure how to dress for dinner at his home. Something casual, she thought, because he'd said they'd be walking on the beach, rather than driving. Pants? Her dark blue skirt? She looked through her wardrobe, decided that none of the clothes she had brought with her would do and that she would go to Torremolinos and try to find something there.

She'd thought a lot about Fernando in the past few days, and wondered where this brief relationship was headed. And yes, she admitted to herself as she dressed for the trip to Torremolinos, Fernando was most definitely a man she was interested in. Not only was he drop-dead handsome, he was probably the gentlest and most considerate man she'd ever dated. Every time he kissed her, her knees all but buckled. That day in the sea, it had been all she could do to pull away. If the wave hadn't separated them, she wasn't sure she would have.

And so she started to think, as Tillie had suggested, about how a long-distance romance might work out. Perhaps, after all, commuting wasn't such a bad idea. Málaga was only six or seven hours from New York. She could fly in occasionally, and Fernando could come to New York to see her.

She smiled as she brushed her hair. Yes, she thought, it just might work out.

In the lobby, she asked about a taxi to take her to Torremolinos. The desk clerk said, "I can call one for you, *señorita*," just as Señor Zavala appeared.

"Torremolinos? No, no, you will not take a taxi. I will have someone drive you, Señorita Fielding."

And, though she protested, he called to one of the elderly men who worked in the hotel and said, "You will drive the *señorita* to Torremolinos and wait for her." And to Kristen he said, "You go to shop?"

"Yes, I want to buy a new dress."

"You are going someplace special tonight?"

"Fernando has invited me to his home for dinner."

"Ah." A strange look crossed Señor Zavala's face. "Well. How nice. Ah, yes. Fernando has a beautiful home. I—I'm sure you will enjoy yourself."

If he was sure, then why did he look so strange? Kristen wondered on the way to Torremolinos. Did Fernando have a wife hidden in the attic, after all? If, indeed, Spanish beach homes had attics. What had caused that look on Señor Zavala's face? Whatever it was, she decided, she'd probably find out tonight.

She found several dress shops in the center of town, away from the beach, and in one of them a dress she thought would do. It was a Gypsy-style dress of cool white cotton, with a ruffled off-the-shoulder look and a full skirt. It fit well, and looked good with her newly acquired tan. She bought a blue dress, too. Not quite so Gypsy-looking, but flowery and feminine.

It was midafternoon by the time she returned to the hotel. She put her packages on the bed and, when she turned, saw the long-stemmed red roses on the dresser.

"What in the world—?" she murmured and, crossing the room, took a card from the small white envelope attached to the vase.

"I look forward with great anticipation to this evening," she read.

"So do I," she said, looking thoughtful. "So do I."

At exactly 7:30, Kristen left her room. Fernando was waiting for her on the patio. "How pretty you look," he said, and, indicating her shoes, asked, "May I carry them for you?"

"Yes, thank you." She rested a hand on his arm to take them off. "Thank you for the roses, Fernando," she said. "They're beautiful."

"My pleasure."

They started up the beach. The night was warm, with only the faintest of breezes coming in off the sea. The moon was full and yellow, and there was a sky full of stars. It was a perfect night for love, Kristen thought, and wondered with a nervous flutter whether that was what Fernando had in mind. And, if he did, how she would react.

They passed several old fishing piers that Fernando said should have been torn down years ago.

"Workmen are supposed to start tearing them down in a few days," he said. "They're an eyesore. The beach will look much better when they're gone."

A little farther on, they came to another, newer, pier. A boat was tied up there, and Fernando said, "My *Sea Witch*. I'll take you out on her one of these days."

Beyond, perhaps fifty yards from the beach, was the house. It was larger than she had thought it would be, stark white, with a red tile roof, low and sprawling and very Spanish.

"How many rooms are there?" she asked, surprised.

"Fifteen."

"Fifteen rooms for only you? My goodness."

He didn't say anything.

There were lights on in the house, and there was candlelight on the patio.

"I thought we'd have dinner out here, if that's all right with you," he said as he took her arm and led her up the steps from the beach.

"Yes, that's fine." Kristen turned to him, smiling. "This is lovely, Fernando. How lucky you are to live here."

And it *was* lovely. The patio was filled with all manner of flowering plants, with palms, ferns and night-blooming jasmine. Music drifted out from somewhere inside. The table had been set with crisp white linen, with china and silver.

A woman wearing a black dress and a crisp white apron hurried out, and Fernando said, in Spanish, "Adela, this is Señorita Fielding from the United States. Kristen, this is Adela Garcia, my housekeeper."

"*Mucho gusto,*" the woman said. "*Bienvenida, señorita.* Welcome."

"*Gracias,*" Kristen answered.

"We'll have an aperitif." Fernando turned to Kristen. "What would you like? A bit of Scotch? A martini? Or perhaps a bit of Manzanilla, one of our good Spanish sherries."

"Manzanilla, please."

He nodded to Adela and, taking Kristen's hand, led her to two chaises that faced the sea. "Later, after dinner, I will show you my house," he said.

"I'd love to see it."

He smiled. "You will."

And again she wondered if he had brought her here with the idea of making love. And, if he had, what she would do.

Adela served the sherry, and a manservant, introduced as Enrique, served a tray of appetizers: *manchego* cheese, small sausage rolls, *jamón serrano* and shrimp.

"No wonder you take time off from your work," Kristen said when she sipped the sherry. "If I lived here, I don't think I'd ever want to leave, either."

If she lived here. Something stirred deep inside him. If, he thought. If. In the glow of candlelight, with that slight smile curving her lips, she looked beautiful, and infinitely desirable. The dress was very becoming, very feminine, and she had worn her hair loose about her shoulders, the way he liked it.

He knew that he wanted her more than he had ever wanted a woman before. He knew, too, how important tonight was to him. And what her reaction would be when she discovered why he had not brought her here before.

When they finished their aperitifs they went to the table. Adela served chilled gazpacho, then salad, asparagus and slices of crispy brown *cochinillo asado* from the small roast pig that Manuela, the cook who had been with him for ten years, had spent the day preparing.

"This is wonderful," Kristen said when she took a second slice of the meat.

"I'm glad you're enjoying it." He poured more red wine into her glass. "But you must save room for dessert, or you'll hurt Manuela's feelings."

"Dessert?" Kristen groaned. "This is all too wonderful, Fernando," she said. "It's a beautiful night, and you have a beautiful home. It's all been so perfect."

"But the night is not yet over," he said, reaching for her hand.

Perhaps now was the time to tell him that, even though she had to go back to New York, she hoped they could see each other again. Perhaps... Something moved from behind one of the palms. The branches quivered, and she heard a sound.

"Fernando..." She touched his hand. "There's... there's something behind the palm."

"What?" He turned, puzzled, then he laughed and said, *"Ven, Carlitos."* And a small boy who looked suspiciously like Fernando came out from behind the palm.

"I thought you were inside playing," Fernando said in Spanish. "What are doing out here?"

"I wanted to see the *señorita.*"

"Then you shall." He put his arm around the boy's shoulders and brought him closer. "This is Señorita Fielding, from the United States," he said. "Kristen, this is my nephew, Carlitos."

His nephew? She held out her hand. "How do you do?" she said in Spanish.

The little boy put his hand in hers, shook it vigorously and said, *"Mucho gusto."*

"Carlitos's parents were killed in a boating accident three years ago," Fernando said. "He's my boy
now, aren't you? And his sister, Lucita, who is eight,
is my daughter."

He had two children. Kristen took a big sip of her
wine.

"Why don't you ask Lucita…" There was a note of
hesitation in Fernando's voice. Then he, too, took a
sip of wine. "Why don't you ask Lucita and the other
children to come meet our guest?"

Other children? There were more? This time Kristen took a bigger sip of her wine. "How…how many
children do you have?" she asked.

"Four." He took a deep breath. "Besides Carlitos
and Lucita. They all call me Tío Nando, but I'm more
than that. I'm their father in every way that counts."

"Oh," Kristen said.

They came trotting out onto the patio—four little
boys and two little girls.

"This is Miss Fielding, children," he said. "Kristen, may I present my boys, Antonio, Hassan,
Ahmed—and you've already met Carlitos."

The boys all shook her hand.

"And my girls." Fernando motioned a pretty eight-
year-old forward. "This is Carlitos's sister, Lucita."

The little girl said, "I am pleased to meet you, Señorita Fielding," and kissed Kristen's cheek.

"And this is Gretyl."

Gretyl, who looked to be about six, hung back.
Fernando motioned her forward, and when she was
closer he put his arm around her and said, "Say hello
to our guest, sweetheart."

"Hola," the child whispered.

She was too thin; her cornflower-blue eyes seemed almost two big for her face.

Fernando brushed the straight blond hair back. "You and Lucita go along with Adela now. I'll see you later, and in the morning we'll all have breakfast together."

"Señorita Fielding, too? Will she be here for breakfast?" Lucita tugged on Kristen's hand. "Can you come for breakfast?" she asked eagerly. "Can you?"

"I—I don't think so." Kristen looked at Lucita, then at Gretyl and the boys, too shocked to say anything else. The man had six children! Dear God, six children!

"Say good-night now." He kissed each child on the cheek, and when at last they turned away, with a last goodbye wave from little Lucita, he turned back to Kristen and said with a smile, "Aren't they wonderful?"

She couldn't even answer.

Chapter Four

He waited for a reaction. She cleared her throat and said, "Well. My goodness. So many children. Where... where did they all come from?"

"Gretyl's from Bosnia. Both of her parents were killed in a bombing raid. Six months ago, a friend of mine who had been working in Bosnia to try to get children like Gretyl out of the country asked if I would take her in. I said yes, of course."

"Of course," Kristen murmured.

"It's been difficult for her. She's only six, and still frightened of almost everything. If the cook drops a dish, she panics. Even when the other children are too loud, she runs for cover." He shook his head. "Poor frightened little rabbit, losing her parents and her home, watching her friends die. The emotional scars she suffered will always be with her, but with enough love, perhaps in time she'll be able to put the memory of what happened in her homeland out of her mind. She'll always miss her parents, of course, but the children and I do everything we can to try to make her feel at home."

"I'm sure you do." How good he was, she thought, how kind. And she hated herself for not being able to respond with more understanding. But learning about the children had been a shock; he should have told her about them before this. But if he had, would she have continued seeing him? She didn't think so.

"I found Hassan in Tangier." Fernando signaled to Adela for coffee, and when it had been served he said, "I was there representing a client in a legal matter. We went to a club one night. It was late when we came out, and it was raining. We couldn't get a taxi, so we had to walk a few blocks toward one of the main boulevards. To get there, we passed through one of the less savory sections of the city.

"I saw this little boy—he was only four—crouched in an alleyway. He was half drowned, shivering and obviously ill. I asked him where his parents were, and when he wouldn't tell me I picked him up and took him to the local authorities. They said he could spend the night in the police station, but I said he needed medical attention, and they let me take him to a hospital.

"It took the police several days to discover that his only relative was an aunt, a prostitute who had no interest in the boy. She'd let Hassan sleep on a straw mat on the floor of the room she rented, but whenever she had a customer she'd shut him out. The boy had no one, really, nowhere to go."

"So you took him." Kristen's head was in a whirl; she felt disoriented, unable to reconcile the man she had come to think of as the perfect bachelor to this man with six children.

"Yes," Fernando said. "Of course I took him. There were legal papers to take care of and it helped that I'm an attorney."

"And the other boy? Was he from Tangier, too?"

"Ahmed? Yes, he's from Tangier. A few months after I'd taken Hassan one of the policemen I'd met when I found him called to tell me about Ahmed. Ahmed is five, the same age as Carlitos."

"And you adopted him, too."

Fernando nodded. "The papers will be final in the next couple of months."

"What about the older boy? I'm sorry, I don't remember his name."

"Antonio. He's ten. A Gypsy. I found him in Granada, almost two years ago. A friend of mine who lives there wanted to go to the Gypsy caves. We watched flamenco for a while, and then Manolo, my friend, suggested we go to a local bar. He said it would be 'colorful,' and it was. Too colorful for my taste. Some of the Gypsies in the bar were drunk. One word led to another, and there was a knife fight. Antonio, who'd been put to work washing glasses, got in the way, and when one of the men hit him I stepped in.

"The boy was hurt, but nobody seemed to give a damn, so I took him to a local hospital and got him patched up." Fernando's face tightened. "There were other marks on him, too, strap marks and bruises. I realized the boy had been badly abused. I stayed at the hospital with him that night, and the next morning, along with a man I knew from the Guardia Civil, I went back to the Gypsy caves, because I figured that was where Antonio lived.

"It turned out that his parents were dead and he'd been living with an uncle, the drunk who'd hit him the night before. The Guardia Civil arrested the uncle, and I spoke to the authorities about taking the boy. It involved a lot of paperwork, more than I encountered when I adopted Hassan and Ahmed. The authorities let him live here, and finally, after a year, I was able to adopt him."

Why? Kristen wanted to ask. Why had Fernando felt compelled to adopt Antonio and the other children? She could understand his taking in his brother's two children, but the other four? Certainly their stories were heartbreaking, but there were agencies, orphanages, for children like that, weren't there?

Because she needed to know and understand, she said, "Why, Fernando? Why so many children, I mean? I could understand if you were married, but you're not. Raising children is a tremendous responsibility, especially when you're a single parent."

"I like children," he said, "and I have enough money to take care of them." He looked out toward the sea. "There are so many of them, Kristen, children without a home or someone to love and care for them." He took a sip of his coffee. "A few years ago I started an organization that I call Children In Peril. Like similar groups, we try to find homes for children. There's a lot of red tape and a lot of travel involved, but in the four years since its inception we've been able to find homes for almost six thousand children. Right now I'm working with the government in

Ethiopia to bring ten children out. I've managed to find homes for all but one of them." He laughed and said, "And then there were seven."

Seven. And how many more? she wondered. Eight? Nine? Twenty?

"But why?" she asked. "I mean, why you? What made you want to do this?"

He refilled her coffee cup, then his, and, picking up his cup went to stand at the railing. For a little while, he didn't say anything, just stood there, looking out at the beach and the sea beyond.

When Kristen joined him, he said, "My brother Alejandro and I were born in Madrid. My parents were wealthy—my father was an industrialist, my mother an actress. She made films all over the world, and my father, because he did a lot of business in the Orient and the Middle East, traveled most of the time. They were . . ." He spread his hands out over the railing. "They were much too busy to have time for my brother and me."

She covered his hand with her own. "I'm sorry," she said.

"I decided early on, if I ever had children, it wouldn't be that way. I'd always have time for them, I'd always love them." He took a deep breath and let it out slowly. "Alejandro was five years older than me. He met Silvia while he was still a student in Salamanca. They were married the year he graduated.

"Alejandro had followed my father into the business, and he took over when father was killed in a rigging accident in Saudi Arabia. My mother died a year later.

"Alex worked hard, almost as hard as my father. He spent less and less time with Silvia and his children, and one day I had a talk with him. I told him he was turning into Dad, and that he should take some time off to spend with his family. And so, at my suggestion, he bought a boat."

Fernando's hands tightened on the railing. "He and Silvia took it out on a trial run. I don't know what happened, nobody does, but there was an accident. The boat exploded. If I hadn't interfered..." His face was haunted, his body tense.

"No," Kristen said. "It wasn't your fault. You were right to tell him to take time off. Be thankful Carlitos and Lucita weren't with them."

"Yes, I'm thankful for that." He turned and looked at her. "I've been wanting to tell you about my children, but we were just getting to know each other. It seemed precipitate to bring up the subject."

"I understand. There was really no...no reason to tell me." She wanted to say more, longed to say more. Because she couldn't, she looked at her watch and said, "It's late, Fernando. I think I'd like to go back to the hotel now."

He had wanted an assurance that, though she might have been surprised, she had been as charmed by the children as he was. It was obvious she hadn't been charmed, obvious she wanted to leave just as soon as she could.

"Of course," he said. "I'll just tell Adela we're leaving and make sure the children are tucked in."

When she was alone, Kristen stared out at the night. She could hear the rustle of wind through the palm trees, the gentle slap of waves against the shore. Suddenly she felt much older than her thirty-one years. Cold and strangely empty. This was a beautiful place, and Fernando was a wonderful man. But a man she now knew she could never be interested in.

There was very little conversation on the way back to her hotel. When he reached to take her hand, she said, "Doesn't the water look wonderful?" and, breaking away from him, ran down to the water's edge.

A breeze stirred the full skirt of her white dress. With the moonlight on her hair, she looked very different from the way she had when she first arrived. She had been so formal then, so stiff, very much the New York executive. She'd softened during the past few days, and he wondered as he watched her who the real Kristen Fielding was.

When they reached the hotel, he gave her her shoes and she said, "Thank you for dinner. I loved your home, Fernando." She hesitated. "And meeting the children."

"I'll have breakfast with them tomorrow," he said, "but afterward you and I—"

"I don't think so," she said quickly. "I have some business calls to make in the morning. I really don't know how long that will take."

"Well, then . . ." He hesitated. "I'll call you."

She smiled brightly. "Yes, do." She offered her hand. Good night, Fernando."

"Good night, Kristen." He seemed about to say something else, but he didn't. He only looked at her, then turned and started back down the beach.

She stared after him and, with something that might have been a sob, hurried into the hotel.

* * *

Kristen had decided when she was thirteen that she would never have children. That had been the year her mother died and she went to Oregon to live with her aunt Mary.

"I'll take the girl, because it's the Christian thing to do," her aunt said. "Better me than that no-account father of hers."

The no-account father had left home when Kristen was ten. Occasionally, at least until she went to live with her aunt Mary and uncle Fred, there'd been a postcard from him. One Christmas he'd sent a card with two dollar bills enclosed. And though he'd never been much of a father, after a week at Aunt Mary's, Kristen had wished with all her heart that he would come to Oregon and take her away with him.

During the five years she lived with her aunt and uncle, she heard a lot about both her no-account father and the sacrifice Aunt Mary had made by taking her in. She heard it when she served tea and the cookies she baked for the meetings of the Altar Guild Society, at Aunt Mary's weekly bridge game, and at every Sunday dinner she cooked. As though she weren't even in the room, her aunt would recount once again the tragedy of her dear sister's death and how, "Because it was my bounden duty," she had taken Kristen in and treated her just as though she were one of her own children.

Eleven children, none of whom had ever lifted a finger to help Kristen with the housework. That was her job, Aunt Mary said. It was only right, since she had been given a home, that she help with the chores.

Kristen got up at five-thirty every morning to get breakfast for Uncle Fred and her eleven cousins. While they were eating, she packed their lunches, and when they were finally out the door she prepared Aunt Mary's breakfast, took it up to her on a tray and then washed the dishes before she went to school.

For all those teenage years, she cooked the meals, cleaned the house, did the laundry and took care of her cousins.

And vowed she would never have children.

She ran away from Aunt Mary's the day after her eighteenth birthday. For two weeks, she stayed with a friend's family in a neighboring town, and when she got a job picking apples she found a rented room.

Once the apple season was over, she worked in a restaurant, first as a waitress, then as a short-order cook. She saved enough out of her salary and tips for a secretarial course. When she finished it, she got a job in Eugene, and in six months had saved enough money to go to New York. There she got a job as secretary to one of the vice presidents of a cosmetics company.

She took night courses at Columbia, managed to get a degree, and when the man she worked for left to form his own company, Bon Vivant, she went with him. She worked hard. She came into the office two hours ahead of her boss and the other employees every morning, and stayed long after everybody left at night. She learned everything she could about the business. Though she longed to have a business of her own, she knew it would take years of scrimping and saving to get enough money to do that.

One day, right out of the blue, she received a letter from a California attorney telling her that her father had died the year before. The attorney had been trying to track her down and finally, through one of her cousins, had gotten her address, and now he was asking her to communicate with him.

To pay for her father's funeral, she thought. But when she contacted the attorney, she was informed that she was the sole heir to her father's estate. Estate? Her father had been a vagabond all his life. What could he possibly have left her, besides a lot of unpaid bills? But according to the lawyer, her father had struck it rich in California real estate.

She flew out to Los Angeles, signed a sheaf of papers and was handed a check for two hundred and fifty thousand dollars.

Six months later she formed New Woman Cosmetics and hired Tillie McGee, who had worked as a secretary at Bon Vivant, as her assistant. She'd worked like a dog for the past eight years to make New Woman one of the top cosmetics companies in the world, with branches in Paris and Hong Kong. New Woman was her baby, the only baby she needed. She didn't want anything or anyone to change her life.

Even if Fernando Ibarra was the most charming, the most *everything,* man she had ever met. He was a pied piper of a man with a gaggle of children, and she, unfortunately, was a woman who had no time for children in her life.

The following morning, as soon as she had had breakfast, Kristen, over Señor Zavala's objections, took a bus into Málaga. She looked in store windows and bought a leather handbag for Tillie and gold filigree earrings for her secretaries.

She had lunch, then went to the park to watch the black swans, with their cherry-red beaks, paddling peacefully along. She strolled the tree-lined boulevard and sat on a bench to watch the people stroll by and the horse-drawn carriages clip-clop along. She had coffee at a sidewalk café, where Gypsy women moved among the tables, hawking shawls, tablecloths and bedspreads.

It was early evening by the time she returned to Santa Cruz de la Palma. There were several messages for her, the man at the desk said. All from Señor Ibarra.

She went up to her room and, after she'd had a shower and changed, went out to the balcony and watched evening come. When the phone rang, she didn't answer it. When it rang again, a half hour later, she began to cry.

The following morning, she called the airline to make a reservation for a flight back to New York. The soonest she could get a seat, she was told, would be five days from now. She took it.

When she hung up, the phone rang. She hesitated, let it ring five times, then answered.

"I've been trying to reach you," Fernando said. "I called several times yesterday."

"I went to Málaga."

"You should have told me. I would have driven you."

"I wanted to shop, and you would have been bored."

"I doubt that." She heard the strain in his voice. "I'm downstairs," he said. "Have you had breakfast?"

"No. I . . . I thought I'd just have something in my room."

"Then I'll come up."

"No. I—I'll come down."

When she put the phone down, her hands were shaking. She'd already bathed, but she went into the bathroom and splashed cold water on her face. Then she put on a pair of white shorts and the T-shirt he had bought her that day in Mijas.

He was waiting at the foot of the stairs when she came down. He said, *"Buenos dias."* And didn't look as if he'd slept any better than she had.

"Buenos dias, Fernando."

"I thought we'd go out for breakfast."

"But I'm not dressed."

"That's all right. There's a little place right on the beach in Nerja. We can go there." Taking her arm, not giving her a chance to say no, he led her out to his car.

She didn't want this, didn't want to be alone with him. He'd want to talk, want to know why she'd suddenly changed.

But he didn't say anything, except to tell her that it would take at least forty-five minutes to make the drive to Nerja.

They spoke very little. He put on a tape but this time he didn't sing along with it.

When at last they reached the small village that was Nerja, he parked under the shade of a sycamore tree and said, "You must be starved."

"No, not really."

He guided her to a small restaurant and led her out to a palm-shaded promenade that seemed to hang suspended over the sea below. "King Alfonso XII called this the balcony of Europe," he said. "The name stuck."

"It's beautiful here," she said, and meant it.

"There are so many places I would like to show you, Kristen. We must go to Granada and to Córdoba. And Madrid. Of course you must see Madrid."

She tried to smile. "Time's running out," she said. "Perhaps someday. . . if I come back . . ."

If she came back. He knew he was losing her. And knew he would not let her go without a struggle.

A waiter seated them. Kristen said, "Just fruit and coffee."

"The same for me, please," he told the waiter. And when they were alone he said, "What is it, Kristen?"

"What?" she said, trying to smile.

"Why have you changed?"

"I haven't changed. It's just. . . well, the vacation is over. It's time for me to go back to work."

The waiter served the coffee; she took a sip. "I've made a reservation," she said, not looking at Fernando. "I'm leaving at the end of the week."

"It's because of the children, isn't it?"

"The children? No, no, of course not." And it really wasn't just the children.

"Do you find it so strange that an unmarried man would want to have children?"

"No. Well, yes. Perhaps."

"I have a big house," he said. "Money enough to take care of dozens of children, and servants to help me. It would be nice if I were married, if the children had a mother figure. But I do the best I can to make them know they're loved."

He looked out at the sea, then back at her. "I haven't married, because I never found the right woman." He smiled. "What or who is the right person for anyone?" he asked. "What draws a man to a woman or a woman to a man? Is it beauty, a good figure? Something chemical? I wish I knew."

She hadn't touched her fruit. She just sat there, trying to avoid his eyes, drinking coffee.

"Perhaps I should have married when I first took Carlitos and Lucita, but I couldn't marry without love, even for them. For marriage without love would be, at least for me, like a sky without the sun."

He reached across the table and took Kristen's hand. "I'm thirty-six," he said. "I've waited a long time, but now—"

"No!" She pulled her hand away. "Don't say it," she pleaded. "Please . . . just don't say it."

"But why not? I know this is sudden, Kristen, and believe me, I would not have spoken now, if you had not told me you were leaving in a few days. I would have given you time—a month, two, as much time as you needed to know how you felt about me. But because you're leaving, I must speak of this now. I care for you, and I think you are beginning to care for me."

"Fernando…" She took a steadying breath. "Yes," she said, at last. "I am beginning to care for you. But this, whatever it is that we feel, wouldn't work out. I have a company to run. I live in New York, and you live here with your—" She stopped. "It just wouldn't work," she finished.

"Because of the children. That's it, isn't it? It's because of the children that you're running away."

"I'm not running away."

"Don't you like children? Is that it?"

"No. I mean, yes, of course I like children. Everybody likes children." She didn't realized she'd raised her voice until the people at the tables near them turned to stare. "That's not it," she said, lowering her voice.

"Is it me, then, Kristen? Is it because you don't think you could ever fall in love with me?"

Fall in love with him? God help her, she probably already had. With the thought of it, the knowledge that it was true, she gasped, as though in pain. Tears welled unbidden in her eyes, and she turned away.

"Kristen, my dear." He covered her hand with his. "What is it? Please tell me."

"Nothing," she whispered. "It's nothing."

"I see." He waited, and when she seemed in control he asked, "When do you leave?"

"Saturday."

"You cannot go until you've seen Granada."

"Fernando, really, I—"

"We'll go tomorrow."

"No, I . . . I can't."

"I'll tell the children today. Adela is a grandmotherly kind of woman. She will be in charge while we're away."

"Fernando, I can't. It's impossible, really."

"Nothing is impossible." He reached to touch her face and lightly caress her cheek. "You have so few days left," he said. "Please spend them with me."

She looked into eyes as green as the sea and knew she could not deny him, or herself.

"All right," she said.

"You'll come to Granada with me?"

"Yes, Fernando, I'll come with you."

"Bueno," he said, and kissed her.

All she could do was hope to heaven she wasn't making a mistake.

Chapter Five

Surely it was a morning the gods had made. The sky had never been more blue. The air was clear and cool, scented with orange blossoms and the sharp salt sting of the sea.

Kristen had little to say when they started the drive to Granada. She had appeared at the door of the hotel as he drove up, wearing the same white silk blouse and dark blue skirt she had worn that first morning. Once more she had pulled her hair back into a tight chignon.

"Would you like me to put the top up?" he asked.

"No, I have a scarf." She put it on, then asked, "How long a drive is it to Granada?"

"That depends. It's only about eighty-five miles, but we go through part of the Sierra Nevada and there are a lot of curves. We should get there in time for lunch.''

''And we'll be back in time for dinner?''

''Of course.''

She relaxed a bit and leaned back against the seat, thinking that, after all, as long as she had only a few more days in Spain, she really should see something of the country.

As soon as they left Málaga they began to climb, rounding curve after curve of the torturously winding road. The view below was breathtaking, a rolling carpet of verdant green dotted with whitewashed houses, fields of yellow daisies and shepherds tending their sheep.

This was Spain as it had been centuries before, and when in the distance Kristen saw a castle, she began to hum a song about faraway places... ''Faraway places I've been dreaming about,'' she sang, ''And... something about castles in Spain.''

''Sing the rest of it,'' Fernando said with a smile.

''I don't remember any more, only the part about castles in Spain. There really are a lot of them, aren't there?''

''Too many to count. Most of them have been converted into *paradors,* and though they have been refurbished and some of them are quite elegant hotels, they retain the feeling of the castles they once were. Convents, too, have been converted and made into *paradors.* There's one in Granada. I thought we'd have lunch there.''

''Castles in Spain,'' she murmured. Romantic Spain.

She had told herself that if she went with Fernando today she would keep things in perspective. Yes, he was charming, and yes, she liked him. So much. So much. But there were just too many obstacles in the way of their ever being together. She lived in New York, he lived here. A long-distance relationship would never work out.

Then, of course, there was the matter of his children. Six children.

He put on a tape, and when he began to sing along with it she turned to watch him through the dark glasses that hid her eyes. With his tanned skin and midnight-black hair, his even features and full, sensuous mouth, he really was one of the handsomest men she'd ever known. And it wasn't just his looks that attracted her. He was a good and decent man, a man with a zest for living. There was only one flaw to this perfect man, and even that was not a flaw, but an infinite kindness of character.

She wished she was different, wished she could tell him his children were wonderful, that she would love mothering them, and that, yes, they could pursue their relationship, because in time it might very well work out.

But she couldn't; she knew herself too well. She knew it would never work.

When he reached to take her hand and draw her closer, she felt a sudden and overwhelming sadness, and was glad for the sunglasses, because they hid her tears.

The sun was warm on her face. She watched the golden fields rush by, breathed in the sweet, fresh air of Spain, and told herself that tonight, when Fernando took her back to her hotel, she would be able to say goodbye with no regrets.

Tillie had been right to urge her to come to Spain, but Spain was almost over. It was time to go home.

At last, after almost three hours of driving, Fernando pulled the car off the road. "There is Granada," he said. "There below."

Nothing in Kristen's experience had prepared her for that first sight of Granada. It lay like a fairyland city in the bosom of green hills and snow-covered mountains, a place of red-roofed houses and of buildings the color of old gold in the sun of the early afternoon. A jewel of a city, once the very heart of Moorish Spain.

"There is the Alcazaba," Fernando said, pointing to a castle below. "It is said to be the most beautiful Arab castle in existence in the world." He reached for her hand. "You must see it all," he said, "for if you can understand Granada, you will understand my Spain."

His Spain. And him?

He stretched his arm over the back of the seat. "There was a man," he said, "a sultan whose name was Boabdil. In 1492, the year Columbus discovered America, the Moors fell after almost eight-hundred years of rule over Spain. They had already lost Valencia, Toledo, Sevilla and Córdoba, and their empire had finally shrunk to Granada."

"It was Boabdil who handed the city over to Isabella and Ferdinand, both of them in armor, before he rode into exile, with the words 'Here are the keys to paradise.'"

"At the gates of the city, he looked back for one last time, and wept. And as though his pain were not enough, his mother killed his soul with the words 'Do not weep like a woman for what you could not defend as a man.' "

"How terrible." Kristen's eyes grew shiny with unshed tears. "How sad."

"That's how it ended," Fernando went on. "And now every day in Granada, at three o'clock, the bell of the Plegaria Tower strikes three times, to remind the city that at that hour on the second day of January in the year 1492, Spanish Islam faded into the silence of history."

"The silence of history," she whispered. And he knew she was beginning to understand this country of his. And perhaps, God willing, to understand him.

He drove carefully back onto the road. "We will see the city later," he said. "But first we will visit the Alhambra, and you will understand why Moorish Spain will always and forever be a part of our heritage."

He wound his way carefully down the labyrinth of narrow streets and up a curving road until they were once again high above the city. When he'd parked, he said, "Come, Kristen. There is much to see."

There was simply no way to describe the beauty of the gardens of the Alhambra, this incredible palace conceived by the Moors as a paradise on earth. Built in the thirteenth and fourteenth centuries, it seemed to Kristen to be more beautiful than a dream, and as peaceful as heaven. There was mystery here, and enchantment and tragedy.

Sunlight reflected on pools of clear, clean water, sparkled off fountains, ran to pools where the odalisques of the harem had bathed. Arched entranceways, carved with lacelike intricacy, led to sun-filled patios and rooms with stalactite domes and honey-comb ceilings.

"I've never seen anything like this." Kristen spoke in a whisper, as though not to disturb this quiet place, spellbound by the beauty, touched by the sadness of the story of the sultan who had wept when he looked back on his beloved city for one last time.

Fernando took her hand. "I'm so glad you decided to come with me today," he said. "I wanted you to see all of this." And more, he thought. So much more.

When at last they left the Alcazaba, they wandered through the gardens of the Alhambra. Spring flowers bloomed with an abundance of color. The trees and shrubs were trimmed and green, and water splashed from center fountains.

He took her hand and led her to a green bench that looked out on a portion of the garden. There were no other visitors, and it was as if there were only the two of them in this quiet place. She closed her eyes and thought of how it must have been those centuries be-fore. Had Boabdil walked here alone that last morn-ing before he turned his city over to the king and queen of Spain? What pain he must have felt as he gazed one last time at the beauty of these gardens. What sad-ness must have been his when he turned his back on the glory of Granada.

"Kristen?"

She looked at him for a moment, and then, with a shake of her head, she said, "Sorry, I'm afraid I was daydreaming."

"It's almost four. We should have lunch. The *parador* of San Francisco is within walking distance. We can have something there."

The outside of the *parador,* made of stone turned tan-gold in the late-afternoon sun, was classically beautiful, and very old. Inside it was a coolness of old stone walls, with high ceilings, heavy furniture, tapestries, suits of armour, sculptured metal chandeliers and a fireplace large enough to roast a wild boar.

As Kristen gazed around her, she felt as if she had stepped back in time, as if at any moment ladies-in-waiting would appear to lead her to her bedchamber.

She moved as though in a daze, mesmerized by the old-world beauty of this ex-convent, still enthralled by the romance of the Alhambra and the story of Sultan Boabdil.

In her mind's eye she saw the palace that had been the jewel of the Arab world, and thought how it might have been so many centuries ago. She pictured herself strolling in the moonlight, saw the pale light reflected on the quiet pools and breathed in the scent of gardenias.

She thought of the gold-tiled rooms, and it seemed to her she could almost see the sultans who had feasted there, surrounded by poets and musicians. She heard the sound of a lute, smelled jasmine and myrrh and incense. She saw the harem women in their gossamer robes, tasted rose-petal jam, and felt her heart flutter with the others' when it was time for one of them to be chosen as the flower of the night.

Beauty and romance and an almost palpable feeling of sensuality raised to an art form had permeated the very air of the palace. She had been mesmerized by it, lulled by the beauty, caught up in the lure of history, in the way it had been and was no more.

Did the blood of the Moors run in Fernando's veins? Had some long-ago ancestor of his ruled over Granada? And what of the concubines who had waited in the harem? When summoned by the sultan, had they feared the night of love that was to come, or gone willingly, eagerly, to his arms?

Dressed in a diaphanous robe and perfumed with roses, the chosen one would be led by a servant out of the harem to a night of ecstasy with a man like no other man. A man whose skin had been bronzed by the sun, a man with hair as dark as midnight. He would feed her pomegranates and figs. He...

"Kristen?"

She looked at him, startled, still caught in her imaginings, and a slow flush crept into her cheeks. "I...I'm sorry. What...what did you say?"

"I asked if you'd like some *entreméses* to begin with."

"Yes, that...that's fine."

He looked at her for a moment. She seemed different somehow, bemused, her face softened, as though by a dream. He touched her hand and, though she smiled, he had a feeling she wasn't really here.

He ordered the appetizers, along with a pitcher of sangria. The *entreméses,* carried to the table by a waitress in a somber gray uniform, proved to be a number of small dishes—twenty-five, to be exact, for each of them—with shrimp, sardines, small sausages, cheese, Russian eggs, ham, chorizo, smoked salmon, olives and all manner of other delicacies.

When Kristen's eyes widened, Fernando laughed. "And what would you like for the main course?"

Then he touched his glass to hers and said, "I hope you're glad you came out with me today."

Her gray eyes softened to a smoky haze and her lips curved in a smile. "Oh, yes," she said. "Oh, yes." She dipped a shrimp into a bit of sauce and held it to his lips. "It's good," she said. "Taste."

He bit into the shrimp, and when he felt a bit of the sauce on his lip, he picked up his napkin to wipe it away. But she said, "No, let me," and he felt the stroke of her little finger at the corner of his mouth. And, holding his gaze with her own, she licked the sauce from her finger. As he had done their first time out together.

He felt a jolt somewhere in his midsection, the hot kindling of a flame. And surprise, because he knew that Kristen was flirting with him, teasing him. He didn't know why, he only knew that if she didn't stop he was going to sweep her up in his arms and carry her off to a quiet place in the shaded garden they had only just left.

She didn't stop. It was all very ladylike, of course—a smoky look, a sigh, a deep-throated chuckle, the brush of her hand against his. A long and slumberous look.

But why? he wondered. What did it mean?

It was almost six by the time they finished. It would be dark by the time they left to start the drive back to Santa Cruz de la Palma.

"It's late," he said. "And, frankly, I don't like the idea of driving the road back at night. If it's all right with you, I think it would be better if we booked rooms here."

"Yes," she said, a little breathlessly. "Why don't you?"

"I'll ask at the desk." He hesitated. "Are you sure you don't mind?"

"I'm sure," she said with a smile.

He was gone for only a few minutes, and when he returned he held up two keys. *"Hecho!"* he said. "Done. Shall we have a look at our rooms before we start out for some sight-seeing?"

She rose and followed him up a flight of stairs and down an arched corridor. There was a somberness here, and she thought of the black-robed nuns who had made their way down these same cool corridors, chanting their prayers on their way to cell-like rooms.

And again, as she had been caught up in the beauty of the Alhambra, she felt herself touched by the quiet mystery of the silent halls.

Her room, when they reached it, was anything but cell-like. It was spacious and beautifully furnished with an old-fashioned armoire, a dresser, two comfortable-looking chairs, a king-size canopied bed, and a huge stone fireplace at one end of the room.

"The nights are cool here in Granada," Fernando said. "It's quite possible you'll need a fire tonight."

"A toothbrush and a nightgown, too."

"We'll get them when we go into the city." He opened a connecting door. "I'll be in here." He looked inside, then, turning back to her, said, "I'm so glad you decided to come today, Kristen" he said.

"So am I."

He moved closer. "You know I don't want you to leave Spain, don't you?"

"Yes, I know."

"I'm only asking for a little more time. Another week, a month." He put a finger under her chin. "Time for us to know each other, for you to be certain of how you feel." He touched his lips to hers. "I already know," he said. "I've known from the first time I kissed you."

He kissed her now, his mouth on hers, his arms strong and sure around her.

She told herself she would back away, even as her lips parted under his, even as the hands that had meant to push him away came up to encircle his shoulders. Even as she stroked the curly hairs at the back of his neck, she told herself that in a moment she would back away.

His body tightened with a desire she could feel, hers softened with a yielding difficult to control. If she did not stop soon, she wouldn't be able to.

But still she did not stop, not even when he began to struggle with the buttons of her white silk blouse. Not even when she felt the touch of his fingers slip under her bra to stroke her breasts.

He kissed her again, and when she felt his tongue against hers, she moaned deep in her throat. He said, "Kristen... *Querida*, if we don't stop now, I won't be able to control what I am feeling."

She leaned back in his arms, and when she closed her eyes she saw again the beauty of the sultan's castle. She heard the whisper of water dripping from an old stone fountain and the music of a lute. And saw herself, dressed in diaphanous pink, reclining on a brocade sofa, holding up her arms to her lover. A lover who would lead her to paradise.

He tightened his hands on her shoulders and drew her to him. He kissed her with a depth of passion that left her shaking and wanting more. His body was taut with desire, and she swayed against him, holding him as he held her.

"Love..." he murmured against her lips. "Oh, love..."

She put her hands on his chest and whispered, "Wait, Fernando, please wait."

His body ached for her; he wanted her as he had never wanted a woman.

Again she said, "Wait."

But why? *Por Dios,* for how long?

He let her go and, fighting for control, said, "Do you have any idea how much I want you?"

She smiled, a slow, sweet smile. "Oh, yes," she said. "I know."

He knew then, somehow he knew, that before the night ended they would be together in love.

And because he knew, he was able to step back and say, "Why don't you freshen up while I call home? Whenever you're ready, we'll go."

"I want to see the Gypsies," she said.

"Then you shall. But we'll go to the Albaicin first, and later to the Sacramonte, the place of the Gypsies."

She touched his face. "You're not angry?"

He caught her hand and turning it kissed her palm. "No, I'm not angry." He kissed her lightly on the lips and said, "Knock on my door when you're ready to leave."

She watched him go with a sense of reluctance. And the sure knowledge that, before the night was over, she and Fernando would be one.

Chapter Six

It was after seven by the time they left their rooms and drove to the section of Granada known as the Albaicin. The narrow streets were alive with Gypsy sellers, a few tourists, and townspeople out for an evening of fun. Small children darted from shop to shop, women with babies in their arms hawked flowers they hoped no one would take and asked for money. The strumming of a guitar mingled with hard rock from a transistor radio.

Flowers spilled from the balconies above, and colored lanterns lighted the way. Silver jewelry and gold jewelry glittered from shop windows, and Gypsy blouses and dresses were on display, as well as fine Gypsy shawls, castanets and high-heeled slippers.

"You must have something to remember Granada by," Fernando said, and though Kristen demurred, he bought her a white ruffled off-the-shoulder blouse and a pale blue silk shawl. "Put them on now," he said with a smile.

And when she whispered that because of her bra she couldn't wear the off-the-shoulder blouse, he said, "Take the bra off. You don't need it."

Kristen hesitated, but then the Gypsy woman who'd sold the clothes said, "Come." She followed the woman into a small room in the back of the stall. There she took off the silk blouse and her bra and put on the white ruffled blouse.

"You must pull it down over your shoulders," the Gypsy said. "Nice shoulders. Let everyone see."

She handed Kristen the blue shawl, and frowned when Kristen draped it over her shoulders to try to hide the fullness of her breasts.

"No, no," the woman said, "you should not hide the *chi-chis*. You must wear the *mantón* so."

She took the shawl from around Kristen's shoulders and tied it around her waist, so that the triangle part of it and the long fringe draped over her hip. *"Así es."* She nodded her approval. "Now you look like one of us. But you must take the hair down, yes?"

Kristen looked at herself in the mirror that hung at a crooked angle on the wall. The woman was right, the stiff chignon looked wrong with the blouse and the shawl, and so she took the pins out her hair and brushed it soft and loose about her shoulders.

When she came out of the stall, Fernando smiled and hugged her. "Beautiful," he said. And to the woman, *"Arretes, señora.* We must have earrings."

Big gold loops were taken out of a glass case, and Kristen fastened them to her ears. Though she wasn't used to wearing big jewelry, when she turned her head from side to side she liked the feel of the big gold earrings.

"Yes," Fernando said. "You're perfect. A beautiful blond Gypsy, ready for a night of adventure." He linked her arm through his. "Now we will go to Sacromonte."

They left the car where it was, and walked arm in arm through the streets to the quarter that was Sacromonte.

In the moonlight, the Gypsy caves, clawed out of the chalky cliffs, were dark and mysterious, breathing with all the life and romance of Spain.

"The Gypsies have lived here for four hundred years," Fernando told her as they drew closer. "Their homes, furnished like any modest homes, are dug back into the rock."

The air was filled with the strumming of guitars, and when they went closer, it was as if each cavelike house were holding its own celebration. There was music and noise, talk and raucous laughter.

They moved farther on, until they came to a raised platform. A man waved them forward, saying, *"Ven, ven,"* and motioned them to two straight-backed chairs.

A woman in a bright Gypsy dress and a man in tight black trousers and a full-sleeved white shirt faced each other on the makeshift stage. The stage vibrated with the staccato beat of their heels, the hoarse cries of *"¡Olé! ¡Olé!"* from the other Gypsies seated on the wooden stage, and the music of two guitars.

A man began to sing as Kristen had never heard anyone sing before. "The *cante hondo*," Fernando whispered. "The deep song."

"Ayeee..." The voice came from the soul, part Moorish, part Spanish. "Ayeee..." It rose from guttural to keening, and the Gypsies on the platform closed their eyes and their palms came together in a rhythmic clapping, faster and yet faster.

The man and woman sat down, and when they, too, began to clap, another woman stepped out and began to dance to the pounding rhythm, eyes closed, bracelet-covered arms raised, a look of intense suffering on her expressive face. She wasn't young, she wasn't beautiful, yet she seemed the very embodiment of woman. Of suffering and love, of passion and tragedy.

Nothing had prepared Kristen for the impact of this music, the drama of the guitars, the sensuous passion in the movement of the woman who danced, the sharp *tac-tac* of her heels against the wooden floor, the click of the castanets.

Kristen reached for Fernando's hand. "It's so much," she whispered. "So wonderful."

"I know." He put his arm around her, and when he looked at her, he drew his breath in, because there was on her face an expression he had never seen before. It was as if she were one with the women, as if she understood the passion and the tragedy the woman sang of.

The moon came out from behind the clouds, like a golden beacon in the night sky. "Look how beautiful it is," Kristen murmured.

"A Gypsy moon," he said. And kissed her lips.

The night grew cold, and she put the shawl around her shoulders and moved closer to Fernando. When he asked her if she wanted to leave, she said, "No, not yet."

The music ended, and when it began again it seemed to her that she could feel it throbbing inside her. The hoarse voice of the man who sang, and the sobbing of the guitars, touched her as nothing ever had. She saw passion in the face of the women who danced, witnessed their pain, their love and their loss.

A waiter passed glasses of Manzanilla among the audience when the entertainers rested. Kristen and Fernando drank and spoke to the people sitting near them, and to the man who had sung the *cante hondo.* Dark-skinned, with unruly shoulder-length hair and a gold earring in one ear, he seemed as exotic as the night.

"You like the flamenco?" he asked Kristen.

"Oh, yes."

"This is your first time in the Sacromonte?"

"Yes."

"You must come again." He looked at Fernando. "She is your *mujer,* your woman?"

"*Sí,* she is my woman."

"You are a lucky man, *señor.*"

Fernando tightened his arm around her shoulder. "I know, my friend. I know."

The man moved on. The music began again, and now, along with the strum of the guitars, the rhythmic clapping of hands and the staccato beat of heels, it seemed to Kristen that she could hear the words "*Mi mujer.* My woman."

When at last they left the Sacromonte, they walked the quiet streets of the Albaicin. The shops were closed now, as were the doors of all the houses, but from somewhere came the sound of guitars, haunting and beautiful.

Fernando, though he had been here many times, was always moved by the beauty of Granada. But never as much as tonight. The night was soft, the air scented by gardenias. And he was with Kristen.

"I'm so glad I came with you to Granada," she said "It's a beautiful city."

"One of the most beautiful in Spain. A poet once wrote, 'Give alms to the blind man, woman, for in this life what greater suffering can there be than to be blind in Granada.'"

"Yes," she whispered. "I understand."

He put his arm around her waist and drew her closer. They kissed there on the quiet street, not with passion, but with a new understanding and closeness, because of what they had felt when they listened to the flamenco.

They found a *tapa* bar, and when they went in Fernando ordered small dishes of shrimp and *bocarones,* cheese and bread, and glasses of good red wine.

It was long after midnight when they found the car and returned to the *parador.* Kristen was pleasantly tired, still in the thrall of the haunting Gypsy music, lulled by the Manzanilla and the wine, and she leaned into Fernando when he put an arm around her waist.

When they went into her room, she saw that the bed had been turned back and a red rose had been placed on her pillow. She crossed the room and picked it up.

"Is this from the hotel, or from you?" she asked with a smile.

"It seemed the romantic thing to do."

She brushed it back and forth under her nose. "That was very sweet, Fernando. Thank you."

"You're welcome." Suddenly he felt like a teenager, awkward, unsure of himself. "You're very beautiful tonight," he said. "I wanted to tell you."

"Thank you."

"I suppose you want to get to bed."

"I'm in no hurry."

He came closer, and when he rested his hands on her shoulders he remembered that she wasn't wearing a bra. All he had to do was slip the blouse down and he would see her breasts, see them and touch them.

His body hardened with need. She was so close, so beautiful. One kiss, he told himself. That was all. If she wanted him to stop, he would.

He said, "Kristen. *Querida.*" And kissed her.

Her lips softened under his. She wound her arms around his neck and stepped closer.

For a moment, he hesitated. Then with a smothered groan he gathered her in his arms. "Oh, Kristen," he said against her lips. "Oh, love."

The shiver of a sigh ran through her. She thought of all the reasons not to do this, and of all the reasons why it seemed so right.

He kissed her again, deeply, passionately. Then there was no more time for thought, for she was caught up in the feel of his lips on hers, the press of his body against her body. Excitement zinged through her, and she felt the heat of desire.

Her mouth begged for more; the need to be closer overwhelmed her. She pushed his jacket off his shoulders and began to unbutton his shirt.

When she did, he pulled the new white blouse down over her shoulders, the way he had wanted to all evening. Her breasts were small, high and firm. He cupped them with his hands and ran his fingers over the rose-pink nipples. She closed her eyes and moaned into his mouth.

"Tell me," he said. "Kristen, tell me you want this as much as I do."

"I do," she whispered. "Oh, yes."

He carried her to the canopied bed and undressed her. When she lay back against the white linen sheet, clad only in her panties, he let his gaze travel over her body. Hands shaking with eagerness, he stripped off his clothes.

Their eyes met, then moved to savor the sight of each other's bodies. How handsome he was, how finely made. Broad of shoulder and chest, narrow of waist and hip. How strong the legs that would soon bind her to him.

He leaned over her, and though his eyes were hooded with desire, he did not hurry. He stroked her cheek and murmured, "I knew you would look like this." He ran his fingers across her rib cage and up over her breasts, and when he heard the intake of her breath, desire like none he had ever known burned through him.

But he wanted to take his time, to savor all of her, to let his eyes and all his senses see and feel all that she was.

He eased the panties slowly down over her hips. How white her skin was where the sun had not touched her. He laid the palm of his hand across her stomach, heard her gasp, then moved to touch the soft triangle of hair and to caress the silken beauty of her long, perfect legs.

Still watching her, he stepped back long enough to hook his thumbs under his briefs and pull them down.

She looked at him. Her eyes widened, and he heard the catch of breath in her throat.

He lay beside her, and when she faced him, he kissed her mouth and reveled in the feel of the whole warm length of her next to him. He kissed her for a long time—deep, warm kisses while he sampled the sweetness of her mouth.

She caressed his shoulders and tangled her fingers in his chest hair. And when he leaned to kiss her breasts, she whispered, "Yes. Oh, yes."

He was on fire, throbbing with desire, yet wanting to wait. He ran a hand across her stomach and the round of her hip, and at last he touched the apex of her legs and began to stroke her there, very slowly, very gently. All the while, he whispered to her in Spanish how much this meant to him, how he had longed to be with her like this.

She warmed to his touch, yielding herself and all that she was, and when she could no longer stand the sweet torture, she said, "Fernando, please. Please, now, Fernando."

He raised himself over her. He looked into her eyes, kissed her mouth, and joined his body to hers.

She gasped at the strength of him, the power and the force of him, and clung to his shoulders when he began to move against her.

And because she had gasped, he murmured, "Is it too much for you? Have I hurt you?"

"No. Oh, no." She lifted her body to his and sought his mouth. Never before had she felt anything like this. Never before had she experienced this freedom of desire. She wanted to shout with it, to cry a million *yes*es with it, to tell him she loved this and him and that *please please please* she didn't want it to end.

He stroked fast and deep, holding her as she held him, for now they were one, reaching, reaching for that final moment.

"Amor," he whispered. *"Amor de mi vida."*

"Oh, yes," she answered. "Oh, yes."

Then no more words, as a feeling unlike any other took hold of her. She spiraled up and up, her body soaring and alive with sexual excitement. She called out to him, clung to him, held him. His arms tightened around her, his body thundered over hers. In a final burst of passion, he cried her name and kissed her with a fierceness that took her breath away.

"Kristen," he said again and again. "Kristen."

Gently, gently, close and trembling, they settled back into each other's arms. He wouldn't let her go. He held her to his beating heart and rained kisses over her face and her breasts. He smoothed the damp hair back from her face and when at last he made as though to move away, she said, "No, stay. Stay a moment."

Never before had she experienced this closeness, this bonding with another human being. It was not just the physical bonding, though heaven knew it had been wonderful beyond her wildest imaginings. It was more than that. A closeness of heart. A true sense of belonging. Love?

That scared her, but then Fernando kissed her again and all her thoughts dissolved into tenderness. She touched his face. She ran her fingers over the planes of his cheekbones, the indentation between his nose and his mouth. The curve of his lips.

He captured her hand and brought it to his lips. "I knew it would be good between us," he said. "But I didn't know it would be like this."

"Nor did I."

He wanted to tell her that after this, after what they had shared, he could not bear ever to let her go. But he was afraid that if he did she would pull away and say words he didn't want to hear.

So, instead, he kissed her. And in a little while it began again.

Once, in the night, she awoke with the words *"Mi mujer"* echoing in her mind. The music of the guitars sang in her brain, and she could hear the hoarse voice of the Gypsy singing his song of love and loss. And again the words *"Mi mujer,* my woman."

With a muffled cry, she turned to Fernando. She kissed his mouth, and when he woke and said, "What is it, love?" she had no words to tell him.

They made love again, and in that final moment she cried silent tears, because she wasn't his woman, because she never could be.

When she awoke in the morning, light had filtered through an opening in the curtains and Fernando was with her, quietly stroking her breasts. She turned to him, and he kissed her. He cradled her in his arms and told her how fine she was and how much making love with her meant to him.

He kissed her breasts, he teased her nipples. He stroked her slowly, gently, and when she began to touch him he whispered his pleasure into her mouth.

When it became too much, when the breath rasped in their throats, she raised herself up over him, glorying in the feel of him, the strength of the hands that held her, the swell and power of him inside her.

She leaned back and, closing her eyes, began to move against him, slowly at first, then faster, as together they raced toward that moment, that one precious moment.

"Open your eyes, my Kristenita," he pleaded. "Look at me, *mi mujer.*"

And she gazed down into eyes the color of the sea, eyes warm with passion and with love. He gripped her hips, and for a moment his body grew still and they waited, suspended in time, truly joined in body and in spirit, waited for the breathless heartbeat of a moment.

"Love," he whispered, and they began to move against each other again, deep and strong and true. He held her with his eyes, and when the moment came he said, "Now, yes, now, *mi pequeña amorcita, mi preciosa Kristenita.*"

And she soared, head back, throat constricted, her body wild and free, as she cried his name into the silence of the morning.

Afterward, she lay trembling in his arms and felt the frantic beat of her heart against his breast. She said his name again and again and knew that for as long as she lived she would not forget this moment. Or him.

He showed her Granada that day; the beautiful sixteenth-century cathedral and royal chapel, the Alcaiceria with its labyrinth of narrow streets thronged with visitors looking for local crafts.

And when Kristen said she wanted to see the Alhambra one last time, they went there and once again walked hand in hand through the beautiful gardens before returning to the *parador* for lunch.

He had phoned his home the night before, and after lunch he phoned again to tell Adela he would return before evening. But somehow the words would not come, and instead he found himself saying, "I'll be back by lunchtime tomorrow."

He went into Kristen's room. She had changed into the white silk blouse, and when she saw him she said, "I'm ready. We can leave anytime."

He didn't say anything as he crossed to her and began to unbutton her blouse.

"What...what are you doing? We have to leave. We have to—"

He stopped her words with a kiss. "Tomorrow," he said. "We'll leave tomorrow."

"But, Fernando, I have to go back to New York. I have to—"

"To kiss me," he said against her lips. "All you have to do is kiss me."

He picked her up and carried her to the canopied bed. He lay her down and though she protested he unbuttoned her blouse and rested his head against her breasts. And knew he wanted to stay like this with her forever.

When they lay naked in each other's arms he kissed her again and again, and teased and touched her until she cried out to him. He came up over her and for a moment he only looked at her. "Ah, love," he said, and joined his body to hers.

Each time they had made love she had thought, it will never be this good again. But each time it was, mind-boggling, bone-melting good. As good as it was this time.

Afterward when they lay in each other's arms he said, "Don't leave me, Kristen. Don't ever leave me. Don't—"

She stopped his words with a kiss, and held him as he held her.

But still he persisted. "I know you're scheduled to leave at the end of the week," he said. "Please change your mind."

"Fernando, I—"

"Please," he said, stopping her. "We both know that there is something special between us. I believe we knew it even before we were—" he ran a hand over her naked hip "—as we are."

"I have a company to run." She couldn't look at him. "I have to get back to New York."

The thought of her leaving hollowed him. He wanted to say, But we have just found each other. We have only just begun. Don't leave me now that I have found you, not after what we have shared.

"Stay another week." He tried to smile. "Stay a lifetime."

"I can't."

He sought the words to tell her how he felt, how much a part of him she had become. He understood that her work was as important to her as his work was to him. He didn't want to minimize its importance, but he wanted to tell her that it wasn't all of life, that love and family and children were the essence of living.

He had waited a long time for love to come into his life, for the woman who would love him as he loved her. A woman who would love his children and understand the work he had committed himself to.

Surely Kristen could not be as she was if she did not feel as he did. She had said once that she was not a casual woman, and he knew it was true; she would not have been like this if she did not care. That was the hope he clung to. Kristen cared. She had to.

They had dinner that night at a small restaurant near the Alhambra, and afterward they strolled hand in hand through the moonlit gardens. And later, of course, they made love in the canopied bed, and slept the night through in each other's arms.

Chapter Seven

"I must have lunch with the children today," Fernando said on the drive back to Santa Cruz de la Palma the following morning. "But I would like very much if you would come and have dinner with us this evening."

"I'm leaving for New York in a few days, Fernando. I should pack, make some calls." She didn't look at him. "It's time I went home."

"You said you'd stay for another week."

"No, you said I should. I didn't say I would."

"Kristen..." How to find the words to tell her what these past two days had meant to him? How much he cared for her? But words had always come hard for him, even with the children. He gave them love and knew that he expressed his love in many ways, but it was difficult for him to say the words.

Because they had never been spoken to him. He supposed that in their own way his parents had loved him. They had given him expensive clothes and toys and sent him to expensive schools. But never once had they said, "I love you, son."

He knew that what he felt for Kristen was love, and he knew how much being with her meant to him. He wanted to tell her, wanted to say those three simple words, *I love you,* to her. But did she want to hear them?

"Please," he said. "For me, Kristen. For us. Stay a few more days."

"All right," she said at last. "I'll stay until the end of next week."

He reached for her hand. A few more days. He had a few more days to convince her of his love and his need, to show her how right they were together.

When they arrived at her hotel, he helped her out of the car. Señor Zavala came out when he saw them and said, *"Buenos días,* Fernando. And you, Señorita Fielding. Did you enjoy Granada?"

"Yes, it was wonderful."

Fernando took her hand and brought it to his lips. "Until tonight," he said.

"Until tonight, Fernando."

"That is one fine *hombre,"* Zavala said when, with a salute, Fernando drove away.

"Yes, he is."

"You like him, yes?"

"Yes," she said. And with a goodbye nod she went into the hotel, feeling strangely bereft at being alone again, and wondering what she would wear to dinner tonight with Fernando and his six children.

* * *

She was just leaving the hotel that evening, wearing the white Gypsy dress she'd bought in Málaga, when someone said, "Señorita Fielding?" and she looked around to see ten-year-old Antonio, the oldest of Fernando's children, waiting for her at the bottom of the steps that led to the beach.

He was a dark-skinned boy with pale green eyes and impossibly long lashes. He handed her a bunch of daisies, some of them with the dirt still attached, and said, "I have come to escort you."

"Thank you, Antonio. And thank you for the daisies. They're my favorite flower."

He nodded, tried not to smile and, taking her shoes, said, "I will carry them for you."

He had little to say after that. She asked him about school. He said he supposed it was all right, but that he could think of other things to do with his time. "I am an A-number-one fisherman," he said. "My days would be better put to use if Tío Nando would not insist I spend all of my time in school."

Then, as though embarrassed because he might have talked too much, he ran down to the shore and began to look for seashells.

He was gangly thin, all arms and legs and angles, but there was already a look about him that told Kristen he would grow into a handsome man.

When he came back, he handed Kristen a shell and said, "Here, this is for you, if you want it."

"A cowrie," she said, turning it over in her hand. "It's beautiful. Thank you."

"How'd you know it's a cowrie?"

"When I was just about your age, my parents took me to Florida. I spent all my time on the beach, picking up shells. I still have a collection of them."

"So do I." He scuffed the sand with his bare toes. "Maybe you could see my collection sometime."

"I'd like to."

"Tonight?"

"Yes, all right."

"Are you going to keep the cowrie?"

"Of course I am. I'll add it to my collection when I go back to New York."

"How come you have to go?"

"That's where I live. I have a job and friends—"

"You could have friends here, too. Tío Nando's a friend, isn't he?"

"Yes, he is."

"And I could be your friend."

She smiled. "I think you already are."

He smiled back, and something, a tiny something in her breast, fluttered.

Fernando and the other children were waiting for her when she and Antonio reached the beach house.

"I wondered where you were." Fernando looked at the boy. "I wondered where you were, too, young man."

"I went to escort Señorita Kristen."

"I see." He ruffled the boy's hair. "Next time tell me before you take off. *Esta bien?*"

"*Si, Tío.*"

The other children were seated at the table. Kristen smiled at them uncertainly and said, *"Buenas noches."*

"Buenas noches," they chorused.

Fernando held out a chair for her. Four of the children stared. Gretyl looked down at her plate.

"Tío Nando likes you," Carlitos said.

Hassan and Ahmed poked each other in the ribs. Lucita giggled.

"It is a pleasure to see you again, Señorita Fielding," Adela, the housekeeper, said. "Please let me know if there is anything you would like."

"I will, Adela. Thank you."

Two maids, pretty young women in starched white uniforms, served vegetable soup from a china tureen.

Lucita chattered. What was it like in New York? she wanted to know. Was there a beach? Did Kristen live on the beach? Was her house as nice as Tío Nando's house? Did she have a *novio*, a boyfriend? Did she like Tío Nando?

Kristen said that New York was a very big city, that no, she didn't live on the beach, and no, she didn't have a house as nice as this one, that she lived instead in an apartment.

"But do you like Tío Nando?" Lucita persisted.

"Yes, of course."

"Are you going to get married to him?" Carlitos wanted to know.

"That's enough," Fernando said. "Eat your soup, Carlitos."

"But if the Señorita Fielding likes you, then you could get married and she could be your wife and—"

"She's real pretty," Ahmed said.

"Eat!" Fernando shook his head at Kristen as though to say, "Children!" She smiled back. Weakly.

The soup plates were taken away, to be replaced by plates with broiled fish, fresh vegetables and mashed potatoes. One of the serving girls refilled the children's glasses of milk, and when Gretyl, who hadn't yet said a word, reached for her glass, she overturned it. A look of horror crossed her face, and she started to cry.

"It's all right, Gretyl," Fernando said. "Everybody spills milk once in a while."

"Hassan does it all the time," Ahmed said.

"Do not! Do not!" Hassan yelled.

"Do too," Lucita and Carlitos said at the same time.

Then Adela rushed in to mop up the spilled milk and scold, "That's enough."

Hassan and Ahmed poked each other again, Lucita covered her mouth to hold back a giggle, and Gretyl continued to cry.

Was it like this at every meal? Kristen wondered. The children weren't unruly—certainly nothing like the eleven cousins she had cared for. Actually, each one, in his or her own way, was pretty cute. It was just that there were so many of them!

And Fernando, as though reading her thoughts, smiled and said, "You've just witnessed a typical family get-together. It's not always this bad, of course. Sometimes it's worse."

Worse? Kristen took a sip of her coffee and tried to smile back.

The children all had healthy appetites, except for Gretyl, who, once she stopped crying, barely picked at her food. Her glass had been refilled, and now she picked it up with both hands, very carefully. But she didn't join in the conversation with the other children, perhaps because she wasn't yet fluent in Spanish, perhaps because of shyness. She watched Kristen, but whenever Kristen smiled at her, she lowered her head.

Poor little thing, Kristen found herself thinking. How terrible to have lost everything, her parents, her friends and her home, to come to a new country, learn a new language and try to adapt to a new family. Fernando treated her with great kindness, but as kind as he was he could never make up for the father and mother she had lost.

After dinner, when the other children ran off to play a Nintendo game, Gretyl lingered at the table. When Kristen tried to draw her out, when she said, "Do you like school, Gretyl?" the child answered with only a whispered *"Sí."*

Other questions brought similar one-word answers, but still the little girl did not leave to join the other children.

Finally Fernando said, "Wouldn't you like to play the game?"

Gretyl shook her head.

"Would you like to show the Señorita Kristen your room?"

Gretyl nodded, but she wouldn't look at either Fernando or Kristen.

Feeling uncomfortable, not wanting to be alone with this uncommunicative child, because she had no idea what to say to her, Kristen said, "I'd really like to see your room, Gretyl." Not sure it was the right thing to do, she took the little girl's hand.

Gretyl's hand was damp, but she didn't try to pull away. She led Kristen into the house, through the large living room, past other rooms, down a long open corridor to another corridor, and finally to a bedroom with twin beds.

She let go of Kristen's hand then and, pointing to one of the beds, said, "That bed is mine. The other one is Lucita's."

There was a dark-haired doll in a bright polka-dot Gypsy dress on Lucita's bed, and a one-eared teddy bear, much the worse for wear, on Gretyl's.

"Who's this?" Kristen asked, picking up the teddy bear.

"Otto. He's mine."

"I bet you sleep with him." Kristen smiled uncertainly. "I guess that's why he looks a little ragged."

"He got bombed."

"Oh." Oh? Was that all you could say when a child told you that her teddy bear had gotten bombed? That the stuffed animal was all she had left from the life she had known?

Kristen had never felt so inadequate, so unsure of herself. She searched for words of comfort, words to ease this child's pain, and all she could say was "I had a teddy bear when I was your age. His name was Bruce, and he—"

"Señorita Kristen?" Antonio stood in the doorway. "Do you want to see my collection now?"

"Yes. Yes, of course." She turned to Gretyl. "Wouldn't you like to come, too?"

Gretyl shook her head.

"Come *on!*" Antonio said.

"Well, then…" But still Kristen hesitated before she said, "Good night, Gretyl. Thank you for showing me your room."

"Good night," the little girl said, her words barely a whisper, as with head lowered she reached for her one-eared teddy bear.

For a moment, Kristen hesitated. Then, very lightly, she rested her hand on Gretyl's head and said, "Good night, sweetheart."

The other children were in the bedroom Antonio shared with Carlitos, and when Kristen went to the desk where the shells were laid out, they crowded around.

There were cowries like the one Antonio had given her, slipper shells and turban shells, augers, scallops in delicate shades of orange, yellow and lavender, cones, whelks and triton trumpets.

"They're beautiful," Kristen said. "This is a wonderful collection, Antonio."

"Is it as good as yours?"

"I'm afraid yours is much better. I haven't been to a beach in a long time, so I don't have any new shells."

"Me and you could go shelling tomorrow."

"You and I," Fernando said from the doorway. He put his arm around Kristen's waist. "It's late, children," he said. "Time for bed."

"But I'm showing her my shells. I've got another whole box."

"She can see them another time."

Antonio stuck his chin out. "I'm going to walk Señorita Kristen back to her hotel."

"No, you're not, you're going to bed."

"But—"

"No buts. Put your shells away and get ready for bed."

"She shouldn't walk on the beach alone. Somebody might get her."

"Nobody will get her. I'll walk her back myself."

"So he can kiss her." Four-year-old Hassan gave a shriek of laughter and fell back on the bed.

"Kiss kiss kiss," Ahmed said, as though it were the funniest thing he'd ever heard.

"That's enough," Fernando said. "Hassan, you and Ahmed go to your room. Antonio, you and Carlitos go to bed." He picked Lucita up and kissed her cheek. "Off you go, *niña,*" he said when he put her down. "I'll come in later to tuck you in. Tell Señorita Kristen good-night."

"Good night, Señorita Kristen." Lucita kissed Kristen's cheek. So did the three younger boys. Antonio pumped her hand and said, "If I didn't have to go to school tomorrow, we could look for shells."

"But you do have to go to school." Fernando frowned. "No more nonsense, Tonio. I want you to get ready for bed. Now!"

He was smiling when he and Kristen started back down the corridor. "A typical night in the Casa Ibarra," he said with a laugh.

Typical? Kristen thought with a shudder. Did he mean every night was like tonight? It wasn't that the children were bad, because they weren't. But with six different personalities, as well as different nationalities, they created a small bedlam. All but Gretyl, who seemed enclosed in her own small world of misery.

"How long has Gretyl been with you?" she asked when Fernando drew up chairs for them at the edge of the terrace that faced the beach.

"Only six months. She's having a hard time adjusting, not just to Spain, but to me and the other children. Adela spends as much time with her as she can, and so do I. She's started in therapy, and once a week either Adela or I take her to a child psychologist in Málaga. We're hoping for a breakthrough, but it hasn't happened yet. Gretyl has been so badly emotionally scarred that it may take years for those scars to heal."

"I know you're doing everything you can for her, and for the other children, too. You've given them a wonderful home, Fernando. You clothe and feed them and send them to school—"

"And love them." He looked at her for a moment before he turned to gaze out at the sea. "Perhaps you don't understand what they give to me," he said. "How barren my life was before I had them. I didn't know it, of course. I traveled. I had friends, women I enjoyed, and work I was good at.

"When Alejandro was killed . . ." He stopped for a moment and took a deep breath as though to steady himself before he went on. "I took Carlitos and Lucita. It was a big adjustment at first. I was used to doing whatever I pleased, and suddenly I had two small children to care for, a little girl who cried every night for her mother and a boy who looked so much like his father it broke my heart.

"Then . . ." He shrugged. "I don't know, the other children just seemed to happen. Antonio came first, then Ahmed and Hassan, and finally Gretyl. And after a bit it seemed the more there were the easier it became."

He leaned back in his chair and reached for Kristen's hand. "The children changed my life in many ways," he said. "My practice was in international law, and my business was mostly with large corporations, international tax laws, import and export, things like that. But since I've had the children, I find that more and more I tend to become involved with laws having to do with children's rights, especially when the children are refugees. I still do corporate law, of course, but most of my time is spent with the interests of children. That's why I formed the Children In Peril organization. Because of it, I travel more than I'd like to, but thank God, I have Adela. She's a Godsend."

"I'm sure she is."

"My life is full." His eyes were intent on hers. "At least it seemed full until I met you."

"Fernando—"

"No," she said, stopping her. "We have to talk about this, Kristen. About you and me and what happened in Granada." He gripped her hand. "We made love," he said. "I think we started falling in love."

"No," she said quickly. "No, I—"

"Don't pretend it didn't mean something."

"Of course it meant something. But we can't... I live in New York, and you live here. It's been . . . nice, Fernando, but—"

"Nice?" he said interrupting her. Was that the word to describe what had happened between them? Making love to him had been *nice?*

"I'm sorry," she said quickly. "I'm afraid I'm not very good at saying what I mean. Of course, what happened in Granada meant a lot to me. It was wonderful, you were wonderful. I'll never forget you, but—'' Suddenly, then, though she tried to suppress them, all kinds of emotions welled up inside her, and she couldn't go on.

"Making love with you, spending time with you, was the best thing that ever happened to me," he said. "It meant everything to me, Kristen, and so do you."

"I have a company to go back to," she said. "Responsibilities."

"I'm not minimizing any of that. Believe me, Kristen, I respect what you do and what you've accomplished in your life."

"We can see each other again, Fernando. You could come to New York—"

"A long-distance relationship?" He shook his head. "I don't think so."

He stood and, taking her hands, drew her up beside him. "I've fallen in love with you," he said. "I want you to marry me."

"Marry?" From somewhere inside the house, she heard a little boy laugh and call out, "Did too! Did too!"

"I can't." She turned away so that he wouldn't see her sudden tears. "My job. Your responsibilities. Your ... your children."

For a long moment, Fernando didn't speak. "That's it, isn't it?" he said at last. "It's the children. You don't like them."

"It's not that I don't like them."

"Is it me, then?" He faced her. "Is it me you're unsure of? I know this has happened awfully fast, but we can give it all the time you need. All I ask is that you give us a chance. Me and my children. Just give us a chance."

"Fernando, I—"

"I have to tell them good-night," he said. "Then I'll walk you back to your hotel and we can talk. Wait for me. Please wait for me."

She stood at the railing when he left. She hadn't counted on this when she came to Spain. All she'd wanted was to get away from New York for a week or two. She hadn't been looking for romance. She didn't want to get married, at least not for several years. And certainly not to a man with a ready-made family.

Fernando was the nicest man she'd ever met, wonderful in every way. And, yes, though she would deny it, she was falling in love with him. But she didn't want to. She couldn't live in Spain. She couldn't be a mother to six, soon to be seven, children. It simply wasn't in her.

And yet... No, she told herself firmly. There is no *and yet*. She couldn't marry Fernando, and she couldn't suddenly become the mother to six children.

When he came back out onto the patio, they started up the beach to her hotel. The night was soft, with the same full moon there had been in Granada. A Gypsy moon, Fernando had called it.

And she knew, in that moment she knew, that from now on, whenever she saw a full moon, she would think of it as a Gypsy moon. She would remember Fernando, and the way it had been in Granada.

He stopped before they got to her hotel and, turning her toward him, said, "I'm not asking you to give me your answer now, Kristen. I'm only asking you to give us, you and me, a chance." He drew her closer. "When two people meet and love happens, it is a gift from God. To turn your back on love would be a sin."

He gripped her hands. "I'm going to ask something of you. I'm going to ask you to move into my house with me and my children for two weeks."

"Two weeks!"

"Two weeks out of your life, to get to know us, that's all I ask. And if at the end of that time you still feel that it could never work out between us, that after all you don't love me, or that you find the children impossible to live with, then I'll let you go and we'll try to get on with our lives."

What he suggested was impossible. Ridiculous. Move into his home with him and his six children? My God, she'd go stark raving mad in a day.

"Please, love," he said.

"Fernando, I—"

He kissed her there in the shadow of the palms. Kissed her until her knees grew weak and a flame curled bright and hot in her belly. And, though she tried to deny him, her lips parted under his, and she clung to him as he did to her.

"Give us this chance," he whispered against her lips. "Please, Kristen."

She leaned back in his arms. His eyes, in the light of the Gypsy moon, were filled with longing, a longing she could not deny. In her heart she knew two weeks wouldn't make a difference in the way she felt, but she could give him that. At least she could give him that.

"All right," she said.

For a moment, he didn't say anything. He clasped her in his arms and held her so close she could feel the wild beating of his heart. Then he held her away from him and said, "You'll come?"

"Yes."

"Tomorrow?"

Kristen nodded. "But you promise, Fernando, you promise that at the end of the two weeks, if I still feel the same way, you'll let me go."

"I promise," he said. And prayed as he had never prayed before, that when the time came for her to leave, she would have changed her mind. That she would never, please God, leave him.

Chapter Eight

The phone rang a long time before Tillie picked it up. "Whozat?" she mumbled.

"It's me. Kris. Did I wake you?"

There was a moment of silence. "Kris? It's three o'damn clock in the morning!"

"I'm sorry. I get the changes in time confused."

"S'all right. Wait'll I turn a light on. Okay, I'm more or less awake. What's up? Something wrong?"

"Not exactly."

"Not exactly? What does that mean? What's going on?"

"You remember the man I told you about?"

"The Spanish guy? Yes, I remember."

"I went to Granada with him."

"That's nice."

"For two days."

"Oh. Like for all night? Like you went to bed with him?"

"Um . . . yes."

"How was it?"

"Tillie!"

"Don't *Tillie* me. Just tell me, on a scale from one to ten, how it was."

"It broke the scale, Til. It was incredibly, unbelievably, mind-bogglingly wonderful."

There was a delighted chortle of laughter on the other end of the line, and Tillie said, "I guess this means you're not coming back as soon as you planned."

"I'm staying two more weeks." Kristen's voice firmed. "Just two more, that's all."

"Then what?"

"Then I'm coming back to New York."

"But what about . . . What's his name?"

"Fernando. Fernando Ibarra."

"What about him?"

"I don't know, Til. I mean, he lives here and I live there." She hesitated. "I told you he has six children, didn't I?"

"Six . . . ? No, actually, Kris, you didn't tell me."

"Well, he does. They're all adopted. Two are his brother's children. Then there's a ten-year-old Gypsy boy, two boys from Tangier, and a six-year-old girl from Bosnia."

"Mother of God!"

"My sentiments exactly."

"You're telling me that this sensational guy, this dream of a man who makes your toes curl, has six kids? How do you feel about that?"

"Don't ask." Kristen hesitated. "The thing is, Til, I mean, why I called you at home instead of at the office . . . well, actually, the thing is that last night Fernando asked me to marry him."

"Marry—? Like till death us do—? Hang on, I've got to get a cigarette before I hear the rest of this."

Kristen waited. She heard the click of a lighter and Tillie's indrawn breath before she said, "So? How do you feel about that? Do you love the guy?"

"I think so. I don't know. I'm confused. He's the nicest man I've ever met. And not just nice, he's wonderful in every way. And when he kisses me . . . God, Til, when he kisses me my knees buckle and my insides turn to Jell-O."

"So what's the problem?"

"I live in New York, he lives here. I'm an American, he's Spanish, so there's a difference in culture." She paused. "And then there're the children."

"Six of 'em."

"Soon to be seven. He's started adoption papers for a boy from Ethiopia."

"Problem time, right?" And, without waiting for an answer, Tillie said, "Somehow, Kris, I can't see you keeping house for seven kids and maybe a couple of your own. Cooking, cleaning, washing all those clothes . . . Sheesh!"

"It wouldn't be quite that way. Fernando has a housekeeper and a cook, servants . . ." She heard Tillie draw in on her cigarette, and wished she hadn't quit smoking. "Last night Fernando asked me to move in with him and the kids for two weeks, to give myself a chance to get to know them better. I don't know what to do. If I do what he asks, I'm raising his hopes, and

if I don't, I'm afraid I'll always regret that I didn't give
it a chance."

"I think you should do it," Tillie said.

"Do you? I do, too, but the whole idea scares me to
death. It's been so long since I've been around kids."

"Then I guess this'll be a crash course." Tillie
laughed. "You must really be nuts about the guy."

"I am." Kristen's voice wobbled. "But you know
how I feel about having kids. You know I decided a
long time ago I wouldn't."

"Because of your witch of an aunt."

"I had enough of kids from the time I was thirteen
until I was eighteen to last me a lifetime. Now I'm
moving in with a man who has six." She tried to laugh,
but her voice broke, and she had to wait a minute before she could go on. "Oh, hell," she said when she
could. "Go back to sleep. I'll put in my two
weeks—"

"You make it sound like a jail sentence!"

"That's what it'll be like, I'm afraid. But it's just for
two weeks, that's all. Then I'll come back."

"But if you love Fernando..."

"I'll get over it." Then, because she knew that if she
said another word she'd burst into tears, Kristen said,
"Go back to sleep, Til. I'm sorry I woke you. I'll call
you later at the office and give you Fernando's number."

"If there's anything I can do—if you need to talk,
anything—you can always call me, Kris. You know
that."

"I know."

When Kristen replaced the phone, she sent down for her breakfast. And when she had eaten, she began to pack.

He told the children that morning at breakfast. "Señorita Kristen is going to stay with us for a little while," he said. "I'll expect all of you to be on your best behavior while she's here."

He wished it had happened two weeks ago, or two weeks from now when they would all be back in school. But *Semana Santa,* Holy Week, was about to begin, and they were on a two-week vacation.

It would have been easier for Kristen, less of an adjustment for her, if they were in school. The little ones were in kindergarten from eight to noon, the older children in school from eight to two. On Monday their two-week vacation would start. He and Kristen would hardly have a minute alone.

He'd had no choice about the time, of course. Because of Kristen's plans to return to New York, it was now or never. If he hadn't asked her, she would have gone back, and he might never have seen her again. It was true that he could fly there occasionally, or that she might return here every six months or so, but that wasn't the kind of a relationship he wanted. He had fallen in love with Kristen, and he wanted to marry her.

He looked at the children. Their small faces were solemn. Antonio said, "Can she go fishing with me?"

"Certainly, if she'd like to."

Carlitos took a sip of his milk. "Are you going to get married with her?" he asked.

"I don't know, Carlitos. Señorita Kristen and I are friends. I'd like very much for her to stay here and live with us, but she lives in New York."

"While she's here she could sleep with me," Lucita said.

"That's very nice of you, Lucita, but I think it would be better if we gave her the guest room."

"What're we going to call her?" Ahmed asked.

"You can talk to her about that." Fernando took a sip of his coffee. "But I think Señorita Kristen would be all right."

"If you get married with her, she wouldn't be a señorita anymore, would she?" the five-year-old Ahmed asked.

"Of course she wouldn't, dummy," Antonio said. "Her name would be Ibarra, just like ours."

"Don't call your brother a dummy." Fernando looked around the table. These were his children, and he loved them, but there were times when they could be a handful. How would Kristen, who'd never had children, who didn't seem comfortable around them, react? If it wasn't *Semana Santa,* he and Kristen would have at least a part of the day to themselves, but it was *Semana Santa* and the children would be here all day long.

But perhaps, after all, it was better for her to see right away what it was like to live with a houseful of children.

He looked around the table. The children seemed pleased at the prospect of Kristen's coming to stay for a while. Except for Gretyl, who hadn't said a word.

When the other children left the table he said, "Come here, Gretyl, I'd like to talk to you for a minute."

She looked alarmed. "Did I do something bad?" she whispered.

"Of course you didn't." He put his arm around her. "I just wanted to talk to you about the Señorita Kristen. I wanted to know how you felt about her coming to stay with us for a while."

"Maybe she won't like me."

"Of course she'll like you, *niña.*"

"But if she doesn't if she stays here forever and you get married with her, she might send me away."

For a moment, Fernando didn't say anything. From the day he had brought Gretyl from the orphanage in Bosnia, he had tried to convince her that this was her home and that she was safe here. But she still had so many fears, so many uncertainties.

And nightmares. Though they had lessened, she still had them at least once or twice a week. He was grateful that Lucita and the other children were sound sleepers, that the cries of terror that came suddenly in the night didn't awaken them. He kept the door of his bedroom open so that he could hurry to Gretyl's side if he heard her. When he had to be away, Adela moved into the guest room so that she could comfort Gretyl. The child had lost both her parents, and she'd been through the trauma of war. No wonder she had nightmares.

Little by little, though, she had begun to adjust. Now someone new was coming into the house, and that frightened her.

He picked her up and put her on his lap. "You're my little girl," he said. "Nothing is ever going to change that. Señorita Kristen is a friend of mine, and I've asked her to stay with us for a while. But even if I marry her and she stays with us forever, that won't change how I feel about you and the other children." He kissed the top of her head. "Besides," he said, "I have a hunch the Señorita Kristen already likes you."

"You do?"

"Yes, I do."

"I showed her Otto, and she said she had a teddy bear named Bruce when she was a little girl."

"Well, then, you see, you and the Señorita Kristen already have something in common." He set her down on the floor. "Being here is going to be a little strange for her," he said. "It would be nice, when she comes, if you showed her where her room is and helped her get acquainted with the house. It's really something a girl should do."

She nodded, her small face solemn. "When is she coming?"

Fernando looked at his watch. "Pretty soon, I imagine. I'm going to call her, and then I'll drive over to the hotel and get her."

"I could pick some flowers for her room."

"That's a wonderful idea, Gretyl. I knew I could count on you."

The shadow of a smile crossed her face, and she said, "I'll go do it now."

Fernando watched her go, and for the first time since he had asked Kristen to move into his home, he felt a moment of doubt, not only for Kristen, but for Gretyl and the other children, as well. Children were quick to give their affection; Antonio already had a king-size crush on Kristen, Lucita was willing to share her bed with her, and Gretyl had shown the first small spark of animation he'd seen since she'd come to live with him.

Kristen would be here in his home for two weeks. Time enough for the children to become accustomed to seeing her every day. What would it be like when she left—for him and for the children?

He had to try to convince her to stay, to marry him. She mustn't think he wanted her to marry him for the children's sake, that he was only looking for a mother for his children. If that was the case, he could have married before. No, he had asked Kristen to marry him because he'd fallen in love with her. He could only hope she loved him in return. And that in time she would come to love his children.

She was at the desk, taking care of her bill, when he went into the hotel. He said, "Well, here you are. All ready?"

She smiled uncertainly. "Yes. I'll just be a moment."

"No hurry." Fernando nodded to Señor Zavala. "I suppose Kristen has told you she's going to be staying with me and the children for a couple of weeks."

"Yes, my friend, she has told me." He chuckled. "And I have told her it would be more quiet here at the hotel. However, I am afraid she has already made up her mind to go with you and your menagerie."

"Six children do not a menagerie make," Fernando said.

"Ah, but you forget, Fernando, I have seen your children." He shook hands with Kristen, motioned to a young man to pick up her luggage and walked with her and Fernando out to Fernando's car. There he took her hand, kissed it and then helped her in.

"If it gets too much for you, come back to us," he said with a grin. "Your room will be ready and waiting."

"Don't count on it," Fernando muttered under his breath as he shot out of the driveway.

"Slow down," Kristen said with a laugh. "He was only joking."

"Some joke." Instead of taking the road that led back to his home, he took a side road leading to a deserted section of the beach. He wasn't sure how much time he'd have alone with her during the rest of the day, and there were some things they needed to talk about.

"There's plenty of time before we have lunch," he said when he stopped. "I thought I'd steal a couple of minutes alone with you before we see the kids." He put his arm up over the back of the seat. "Usually they're in school all week."

"Usually?"

He nodded. "The little ones are in *kinder*—kindergarten—and the older ones go from eight until two. But this is the beginning of *Semana Santa,* Holy Week, so they'll be home."

"All the time?"

"I'm afraid so." He ventured a smile. "I thought I'd better warn you. I guess there's nothing like jumping right into it."

She swallowed. "I . . . I guess not."

"We'll go out to dinner as often as we can—just the two of us, I mean. Manuela—she's the cook—and Adela will make sure the children are taken care of." He curled a strand of hair around his finger. "There's something else, Kristen. About us. I thought you might be more comfortable in your own room. Naturally, I'd like us to be together, but I don't want to put any pressure on you. I just thought that because of the children you might prefer your own room."

"Yes, I would." She hesitated. "Did you tell them I'm coming to stay for a little while?"

"Yes, at breakfast this morning. Antonio wants you to go fishing with him, and Lucita offered to let you sleep with her. Gretyl was afraid you wouldn't like her, but when I told her I was sure you already did, she said she'd pick some flowers for your room."

He took her hand. "I know you're probably not used to children, Kristen, but they really are good kids."

"I'm sure they are."

"We'll manage some time alone." He smiled. "I plan to send them to bed as early as I can."

She smiled back. But it was tentative smile, and he knew she wasn't looking forward to the next two weeks.

He tugged on the strand of hair to draw her closer. "Would you mind very much if I kissed you?"

"Not . . . very much."

He brushed his lips across hers, at first tentatively, sampling a bit, then backing away to look into her eyes, to let his gaze slowly lower to her mouth, before he kissed her again.

Her arms crept up around his neck, and when he drew her closer, her lips parted.

The kiss deepened. Their breathing became ragged, frantic, fast.

She was suffused by heat, and by a longing that made her whimper her desire against his lips. He cupped her breasts, and she moaned into his mouth. He ran his thumbs across her nipples and she said, close to weeping, "Oh, don't. Please don't."

He hesitated, then stopped, because he knew he had to. Knew there could be no culmination of their desire. Not here. Not yet.

She put her hands against his chest. "We can't do this," she whispered.

For a moment, he couldn't even speak. "I know," he said at last. "I only meant to kiss you, Kristen. Just a little kiss."

"I only meant to kiss you back. Just a little kiss."

They smiled at each other, and he said, "You carry one hell of a wallop, woman."

"So do you, Señor Ibarra."

"I'm going to have a hard time keeping my hands off you in front of the kids."

The kids. That cooled her off.

"I guess we'd better get going." He started the car. "They're waiting lunch for us."

Lunch. She thought of last night's dinner and tried not to shudder, tried to summon a smile when she said, "Lead on, *señor.*"

And wondered how she would survive the next two weeks.

Chapter Nine

The children, lined up like small steps, were waiting in the front room when Fernando opened the door and ushered Kristen into the house.

Lucita, doll-like in a white pinafore, with her black hair in braids, her big dark eyes twinkling with curiosity, bobbed her head and bent one knee in a curtsy.

The three smaller boys, dressed in shorts and shirts, looked scrubbed clean and eager. As did Antonio. His black hair was wet and slicked back, and his white shirt and dark trousers were immaculate.

They were all dark-haired, dark-eyed children, except for blond and blue-eyed Gretyl. Dressed in a gray skirt and dark blue blouse that did nothing to add color to her face, she seemed out of place and ill at ease here with these eager and active children.

Fernando led Kristen forward. With a sweep of his

arm, he said, *"Bienvenido* to the Casa Ibarra."

"Thank you." She looked at the children. They looked back at her. *"Buen—Buenas tardes,"* she said.

"Buenas tardes," they repeated in unison.

Fernando put her suitcases down just as Adela appeared, followed by a man and a woman Kristen hadn't seen before, along with the two serving girls.

"You already know Adela," Fernando said. "This is Manuela, who cooks for us." He indicated a short, round, pleasant-faced woman with snapping black eyes and dark braids wound around her head. "And her husband, Enrique, who does all sorts of things around the house."

Enrique, as tall and thin as Manuela was short and round, bowed from the waist and said, "We are at your service, Señorita."

"Thank you."

"And Consuelo and Carmelita," Fernando went on. "They live in the village. We couldn't do without them."

Kristen said, "How do you do?" and they all shook hands with her.

"Perhaps you'd like to get settled before we have lunch," Fernando said. "Enrique will take your bags."

"I can take her bags." And as though to prove he was quite capable of handling them, Antonio picked both bags up before Enrique could step forward.

"I can help," five-year-old Carlitos said, and tried to take the largest of the bags away from Federico.

"You're too little."

"No, I'm not!"

The two boys struggled with the biggest bag. Carlitos's face was red with the effort, Antonio's with anger.

"Let go!" he cried.

"*You* let go!"

Fernando stepped between them. "Put the bags down, both of you," he ordered in a no-nonsense voice. "Enrique will take them."

Carlitos let go and, with an enraged cry and small fists flailing, flung himself at Antonio.

Fernando picked him up by the seat of his pants. "Stop this at once," he said. "Carlitos, go to your room and wait until you're sent for. Antonio, I want you out on the patio in your place at the table until the rest of us come out for lunch. I'm ashamed of both of you, fighting like this in front of the Señorita Kristen."

Tears stung Carlitos's eyes. He started to protest, then, with a sob, ran out of the room. Antonio's cheeks blazed with embarrassment, but he, too, did as he was told.

"Boys." Lucita looked up at Kristen and shook her head. "They just don't know how to behave, do they?" Then: "Carlitos is crying. Maybe I'd better go make sure he's all right."

"Yes, maybe you had," Fernando said. "Gretyl will show Señorita Kristen to the guest room, won't you, Gretyl?"

Gretyl bobbed her head. She looked up at Kristen, then down at her shoes.

"That would be nice," Kristen said as she followed the little girl out of the room.

The guest room, two doors down from Gretyl's and Lucita's, was as large as Kristen's living room back in New York. The walls were a pale shade of turquoise. The window shutters opened onto the garden, and the white ruffled curtains had been drawn back to let in the noonday sun. The carpet, of a darker turquoise, was thick and soft. A white lace spread covered the queen-size bed at one end of the room. There were two comfortable chairs on either side of the fireplace, a lemon-yellow chaise near the windows, a desk, and a bouquet of sunflowers on the dresser.

"What pretty flowers!" Kristen said.

"I picked them."

"You did? They're lovely, Gretyl." Thinking to give the little girl a thank-you hug, Kristen started toward her. But when she did, Gretyl stepped back. Kristen stopped. "I really like them," she said. "Thank you."

"De... de nada."

She looked shyly up at Kristen, all the while twisting a lock of her hair around and around one finger. Kristen searched for the words to draw her out. There'd have been no problem with the talkative Lucita, but with Gretyl, withdrawn and silent as a mouse, conversation became difficult.

Why, she found herself thinking as she looked around the room, had Fernando brought her here? She was far more comfortable in a boardroom than she was with children. What in the world was she to say to this uncommunicative child? Her only experience with children had been when she herself was very young.

Because of the housework she'd been forced to do, she'd had little time to get close to her cousins. The smaller ones, even though they'd never been taught to pick up after themselves, had been easier. But the older children had treated her like a servant, ordering her about, leaving dirty clothes scattered around the floor, along with stale, half-eaten sandwiches and moldy doughnuts. They'd thrown crumpled bags of potato chips under the bed and spilled soft drinks on the rug, all of which, though she was only a child herself, she'd had to clean up.

She looked at Gretyl. Gretyl looked shyly back at her. "I have to wash my hands before we have lunch," Kristen said. "Do you want to wait for me?"

Gretyl nodded, then went to sit in one of the chairs at the side of the fireplace. She looked very small in the big chair. Although of good quality, the gray skirt and the dark blue blouse that buttoned up the back didn't fit her well. The outfit was too sedate for a little girl. Her hair was at an awkward length, neither short nor long, and her small face was somber and sad.

Kristen looked at her for a moment, hesitated, then went into the bathroom. By the time she came out, Enrique had brought her bags in and Consuelo, the younger of the serving girls, had started to unpack for her.

"Señor Ibarra said to tell you lunch was ready, Señorita Fielding," Consuelo said. "Do not worry about your clothes. I will unpack for you."

"*Gracias, Consuelo.*"

For the next two weeks, she'd be speaking Spanish; thank God she'd taken those night courses.

She looked at Gretyl and said, "You're my guide. I'm depending on you to lead the way so I don't get lost."

Her only answer was a ghost of a smile.

Lunch was a repetition of last night's dinner, only this time it was Ahmed who spilled his milk, and Lucita who broke into tears, because Fernando insisted she finish her vegetables before having her dessert of ice cream with chocolate sauce.

Antonio called her a crybaby, and Carlitos, still stung from the ignominy of being sent to his room, and determined to defend his sister, picked up a roll from the basket on the table and threw it at Antonio.

"That's it!" Fernando jumped up, hauled the five-year-old up out of his chair and said, "You're going back to your room, and you'll stay there until dinnertime. There'll be no dessert, no Nintendo, and no television tonight."

"You hate me!" the little boy cried. His chin wobbling, he looked at Kristen, who had just taken the first bite of her ice cream. "I want my ice cream!" he wailed.

"When you learn to behave." With his hand on the five-year-old's shoulder Fernando propelled him toward the corridor. "March!" he said.

And Carlitos, with a last look at Kristen's dish of ice cream, ran out of the room.

Fernando turned to the older boy. "Antonio, I want you to apologize to Lucita for calling her a crybaby."

Antonio looked down at his plate. "I apologize," he mumbled.

The rest of the lunch, what there was of it, was eaten in silence. Even Hassan, who sucked his thumb between bites, and Ahmed were quiet. Gretyl ate her ice cream without once looking up from her plate.

Were all the meals going to be like this? Kristen wondered. And if they were, how could she possibly live through the next two weeks?

"I've got to go to my office in Málaga," Fernando said when lunch was over and they were alone. "Would you like to ride along with me or would you rather stay here?"

"I'll go with you," she said, so quickly he laughed.

"I'm sorry the children behaved badly. You're part of it, you know. Antonio has a king-size crush on you, and now, I'm afraid, so does Carlitos." He kissed her. "It's your fault that no male between five and a hundred and five can resist you."

He kissed her again and, when he let her go, said, "Hopefully they'll calm down by tomorrow. If they don't, I'll hang them all from hooks in their bedrooms or lock 'em in the attic." He grinned. "Too bad I don't have an attic. We'll have to plan something with them. Maybe we'll take the boat out for a day or two."

On the boat with six children? Terrified that one of them might fall overboard? God help her!

With all her heart, she wished she hadn't agreed to spend these two weeks with Fernando and his children. Wished she could think of an excuse to repack her bags and steal away in the night. But she had committed herself; all she could do now was grin and bear it.

"This will take an hour or so," Fernando said when he ushered her into his office on the sixth floor of an old and beautiful building. "Do you want to wait, or would you like to go out and walk around?"

"I think I'll go shopping."

"Fine. Come back in an hour, and I'll be ready." He put his arms around her. "Thank you for agreeing to stay with us, Kristen. I wanted you to see how we lived, to get to know the children." He rested a hand on her cheek. "And me," he said.

She wanted to tell him then that it wouldn't work. Perhaps if there weren't the children, the two of them might have had, in time, a future together. Fernando was a wonderful man, an admirable man. But a man who loved children. She didn't. That was it. Period. The fault lay with her, and there wasn't a damn thing she could do about it.

When she left him she window-shopped down the tree-lined Paseo del Parque. The stores here were elegant, and in one of them she saw a belt she thought would look good with her blue skirt. She went in to buy it, then a colorful silk scarf, and, thinking to buy some Spanish perfume for Tillie, moved farther on into the store.

When she passed the children's section on her way to the perfume, she saw that the girls' clothes were bright and pretty. She thought of the dark blue blouse and gray skirt Gretyl had worn today and stopped for a moment to look. When a clerk approached to ask if she could help with anything, she said, "Oh, no. I'm only looking."

The clerk motioned toward the little-girl dresses on one of the racks. "Aren't these pretty?" she said. "They're our spring collection. They've just come in."

"I really don't have the time..." She touched one or two of the dresses. And again she thought of the gray skirt and dark-blue blouse Gretyl had worn today. It really wasn't her business, but perhaps she could suggest to Fernando that brighter things be bought for the little girl.

"Isn't this pink sweet?" the saleslady asked.

It was a pale pink cotton with a white collar and puffed sleeves. Kristen hesitated. It would be overstepping for her to buy Gretyl's clothes. Wouldn't it? On the other hand... "What size is it?" she asked.

"The sizes are different here than in the United States," the woman said. "But it will fit a six- or seven-year-old."

She thought of how it would look on Gretyl, how the pink would brighten her complexion. She said, "I don't think so." She even started to walk away. Then she came back and said, "All right. I'll take it." And found herself adding, "Can you show me some skirts and blouses?"

She bought a white ruffled blouse and a short red skirt and, knowing she shouldn't give something to Gretyl without buying something for Lucita, bought a bright blue blouse and a blue hairband for the other little girl, along with a red hairband for Gretyl.

"I hope it's all right," she told Fernando when she met him at his office. "I don't want to overstep, but honestly, the skirt and blouse Gretyl had on today were pretty awful."

"I know. Adela buys all the children's clothes. Lucita knows what she wants, but Gretyl takes whatever Adela picks out for her."

He put his arm around her shoulders. "It was nice of you to think of her, Kristen. Thank you."

"My pleasure," she said. And felt as if she were smiling inside, because it really had given her pleasure to buy a present for the little girl.

"I'm going to take you out to dinner tonight," Fernando said. "Somewhere fancy, somewhere where we can dance."

"I'd like that," she said, remembering the chaos at lunch. "I'd like it a lot."

The other children, all except Gretyl, and Carlitos, who was still restricted to his room, were playing on the beach in front of the house when Kristen and Fernando returned.

"Where's Gretyl?" Kristen asked Adela.

"In her room, I think." The housekeeper shook her head. "She's been here a while now, Señorita Kristen, and she still can't seem to adjust. Perhaps in time, yes?"

"Yes, I hope so."

Packages in hand, Kristen went down the hall to the bedroom the two little girls shared. The door was open. Gretyl was sitting in a chair by the window, looking out at the beach where the other children were playing.

Kristen knocked, and when Gretyl turned she said, "Hi. May I come in?"

Gretyl nodded.

"I brought you some presents." Kristen put two of the packages on Gretyl's bed and the other package on Lucita's bed. "Would you like to open them?"

The little girl, clutching her one-eared teddy bear, came hesitantly toward her.

"I'll hold Otto for you." Kristen handed her the bag with the pink dress. "I hope you like this."

Solemn blue eyes looked into Kristen's. Gretyl handed her the bear, then opened the bag.

"It's a dress," she said.

"Yes."

"It's got puffed sleeves."

"That's what I liked best when I was a little girl. I wanted all my dresses to have puffed sleeves."

"It's pretty."

"So are you. That's why I thought you should have a pretty dress." Kristen reached for the other package and handed it to Gretyl. "The blouse has puffed sleeves, too," she said.

Gretyl's blue eyes widened. "This is for me, too?"

"Yes, it is. And so is the skirt."

"Could I put them on now?"

"Of course. Would you like me to help you?"

"Maybe you could undo the buttons in the back."

She turned around, and Kristen began to unbutton her dark blue blouse. There was a cotton undershirt under it, but even so, Kristen could see the thin little shoulder blades and the delicate bones of the child's spine.

She had a sudden, almost uncontrollable, urge to pull Gretyl to her, to put her arms around the small body and tell Gretyl she would always be safe, that she would never let anything happen to her.

But she didn't. She only helped Gretyl off with the blouse and the gray skirt and, when she put on the new blouse and skirt, took the child's hand and led her into the bathroom. There was a mirror over the sink, and one behind the door.

Gretyl looked at herself. The shadow of a smile softened her lips. ''These are beautiful,'' she said breathlessly. She tried to smooth her hair. ''Maybe if I wet my hair it'd look better.''

''We could brush it back and put the band on. I mean, if you'd like to. Would you like me to brush your hair?''

''If you want to.''

They went back into the bedroom, and Kristen took a hairbrush off the dresser closest to Gretyl's bed. Sitting down on the bed, she motioned Gretyl to her. ''You have such pretty hair,'' she said.

''It's the same color as yours.'' Gretyl reached her hand out and touched Kristen's hair. ''That's the color of my mother's hair,'' she said.

Something knotted in Kristen's throat. ''I bet your mother was as pretty as you are,'' she managed to say.

Gretyl didn't answer, only hung her head. But she moved closer to Kristen, and when they left the room she reached for Kristen's hand.

Be careful, Kristen told herself. Remember you're only going to be here for two weeks. You mustn't let her get too attached to you. Or you to her.

And later, when Fernando asked if she'd like to go with him to tell the children good-night, she said, ''I don't think so.''

''Lucita and Gretyl might like it if you did. Especially Gretyl. She's thrilled with the new clothes you bought her.''

''No, I . . . I want to change before we go out. You go ahead.''

And when he looked at her a little strangely, she tried to smile. "Maybe tomorrow night," she said.

They went to a beachfront restaurant for dinner, a quietly elegant place with pink linen tablecloths, candlelight and music and waiters who wore white gloves.

Kristen wore a black silk dress that ended a few inches above her knees and dipped to a low vee in the back, high-heeled black pumps and sheer black stockings.

Fernando ordered champagne and caviar. "Your reward for putting up with us for lunch," he said.

"It wasn't that bad," she lied. And, taking a sip of her champagne, said, "I'm glad you finally let Carlitos out of his room. He seemed very quiet, didn't he?"

Fernando laughed. "That lasted until bedtime. By the time I went up to tell him and Antonio good-night, he was just as rambunctious as ever." He put a bit of caviar on a cracker and handed it to Kristen. "Carlitos is very much like his father," he said. "Alejandro and I used to fight the way Carlitos and Antonio do, but if anybody else tried to take me on, he'd fly into them."

"You miss him, don't you?"

"All the time, Kristen. There are things I want to tell him about his children, how much Carlitos looks like him, how sweet and cheerful Lucita is." He reached across the table for her hand. "I wish he were here so I could tell him how I feel about you."

"Fernando—"

"He'd be crazy about you," he went on. "He'd say, 'Don't let her get away, *mano*.' And I'd say, 'Don't worry, I don't intend to.'" He stood and, taking her hand, said, "Come and dance with me."

There was something incredibly sexy about dancing with a Latin man to Latin music. He held her close, one hand against the small of her back, the other hand clasped in his, against his chest.

They didn't speak. They didn't need to. Their bodies said it all.

The hand against her back urged her closer. Her body warmed, softened, yielded. He put his face against hers and nuzzled her neck.

"You smell so good," he whispered, his breath hot against her skin. His hand moved to stroke her bare back; he didn't think she was wearing a bra.

She closed her eyes, giving herself up to the music and to him, molding her body to his. He kissed the side of her face, whispering her name. "Kristen. *Querida*. Dearest."

The music stopped, and still they stood with their arms around each other. His eyes were as green as the sea, hers were gone smoky with desire.

They went back to the table. The waiter served their chateaubriand. They barely touched it.

"Let's get out of here." Fernando reached for her hand. It trembled in his.

"Yes," she whispered. "Oh, yes."

He put money on the table. The waiter said, "I'll get your bill, sir."

"No, it's all right." Fernando put his arm around Kristen's waist, and she swayed against him.

In the car, they reached for each other and kissed, kissed until they were breathless, until he said, "We've got to get out of here."

He started the car and shot out of the driveway, and when they were on the highway he pulled her close to him. "I told myself we wouldn't do this. I don't want you to think that I invited you to the house just because I wanted to make love to you." He rubbed her thigh, tightening his hand on the silky sheerness of her stockinged leg. "But I do," he whispered. "*Por Dios,* I do."

She tried to hold herself back, to tell herself that this wouldn't be good for either of them, that it would be better, wiser, if they didn't make love again.

"Take your stockings off."

"Fernando—?" Her heart pounded. "We...we shouldn't," she protested. Even as she started rolling her stockings down over her thighs.

He caressed her bare skin. "You're so soft," he murmured. "You feel so good."

Her body warmed. She moved closer and leaned her head against his shoulder.

The miles flew by. He drove fast. Too fast. Not fast enough.

They reached the house. He ran around to open her door, to help her out, to pull her toward him, to kiss her with an intensity that left her feverish with desire.

"The study." He put his arm around her waist. "We'll go to the study."

Down the long, quiet corridor. Into a room she hadn't been in before. He locked the door before he snapped on a light on over the desk. There were books here, comfortable chairs, a brown leather sofa.

He said, "Oh, love... Oh, Kristen..."

When they kissed, she pushed his suit jacket back off his shoulders. He said, "Wait," then took off his jacket and ripped his shirt up out of his trousers. She pulled the black dress over her head. She wasn't wearing a bra, only skimpy little panties and her black high-heeled pumps.

He kissed her again and, picking her up, carried her to the sofa and laid her gently down. He kissed her breasts, took off her high-heeled pumps and the skimpy little panties and he said, "I can't wait. *Amor de me vida,* I can't wait."

He came over her, into her. A smothered cry escaped her lips and she said, "Yes. Oh, darling, yes..."

For a moment he thought he could not stand the almost unbearable pleasure of being with her like this. Or the way she lifted her body to his, her wonderful abandon, the heat of her desire.

She was everything, all women, the only woman he wanted, now and forever. He tried to tell her with his body, with his kisses, tried to say all the things that were in his heart. *I love you, I adore you. There will never be another woman for me. Only you. Only you.*

She held him with her arms and whispered her passion against his mouth. And when she said again, "Oh, darling, yes... Like that, yes..." he could no longer hold back. He plunged against her like one who had lost all his senses, merging his body with hers, becoming a part of her, as she surely was a part of him.

She was gasping now, whispering his name in a frenzy of desire, soaring against him when he said, "Give me your mouth." And when she did, he cried a cry that came from his very soul. And collapsed against her breast.

They held each other close. But she turned her head so that he wouldn't know when she began to weep her silent tears.

Chapter Ten

Kristen came awake abruptly, uncertain for a moment what had awakened her or where she was. In the faint light of the moon, she saw the white curtains moving in the offshore breeze.

And remembered the loving. Remembered that after they made love, Fernando had walked her to her room and said, "I want so much to sleep all night with you in my arms."

"I know."

He kissed her and, with a last lingering look, went down the corridor to his own room.

She smiled and burrowed her head in the pillow, drifting on the edge of sleep. She was almost asleep when she heard the cry. She opened her eyes and looked at the bedside clock. Two-thirty. What in the world?

"No no no no!" Cried out in terror. "No!"

She threw back the sheet and sat up. Gretyl, she thought. And, wearing only a nightgown, ran out of the room.

The door to Gretyl's room was ajar. There was a muffled scream, the sound of sobbing. She said, "Gretyl?" and, when there was no answer, hurried to the little girl's bed.

Gretyl rolled from side to side, her face was contorted with fear, crying, "Mama! I want Mama!"

Kristen sat on the bed beside her. "Gretyl? Honey, wake up." She touched the child's shoulder. "You're having a bad dream, Gretyl." She glanced at the other bed. Lucita mumbled in her sleep, but she didn't awaken.

"Shh, baby," she whispered to Gretyl, and raised the six-year-old up and into her arms. "Wake up, Gretyl," she crooned softly. "Wake up, honey. I'm here."

Gretyl gasped and, with a cry, flung her arms around Kristen's neck. Her face was wet with tears, and she shivered with remembered terror.

"It's all right," Kristen whispered. "You're safe now. Don't cry. I'm here. I'm here."

"I got bombed." She hiccuped. "We all got bombed."

"I know, baby. I know." Kristen rubbed the little girl's back and held her close. "It's over now, Gretyl. There aren't any more bombs. You're safe here. Nothing's going to harm you here."

Kristen held the child like that for a long time, soothing her with whispered words, stroking her hair, and when finally the shivering stopped, she laid Gretyl back down.

"I lost Otto." Gretyl sniffled. "Where's Otto?"

"He fell on the floor." Kristen picked him up. "Here he is."

Gretyl clasped him in her arms. "Could you stay for a minute?"

"Of course." Kristen smoothed the hair back from Gretyl's forehead. "You go back to sleep. I'll be right here."

Gretyl's eyes drifted closed. "Mama, sing to me," she whispered.

"But I'm not..." She looked at the little girl's tear-streaked face and, because it was the only song she could think of, she began to sing, in English, "Casey would waltz with a strawberry blonde..."

A smile softened the small face.

"And the band played on..." Kristen softly sang as she stroked Gretyl's hair.

She sat there, singing when she remembered the words, humming when she didn't, even after she knew Gretyl was sleeping. When at last she stood, she looked at Lucita to make sure she was still sleeping. Then, reluctant to leave, she stood for a moment beside Gretyl's bed and, leaning down, she brushed a kiss across the child's forehead.

And Fernando, who had been standing in the doorway, stepped back into the shadow of the corridor.

He had known when they were in Granada that he was beginning to fall in love with Kristen. She was beautiful, elegant and every inch a woman. It puzzled and hurt him that she drew away from his children.

She was pleasant to them, of course, but only just that.

He still remembered the expression on her face when she'd realized he had six children, soon to be seven, because in the next few weeks the little boy from Ethiopia would join the family.

There were many obstacles to overcome; her living in New York, her work there, perhaps even a basic difference in culture. But what if the biggest obstacle was the children? What if Kristen couldn't accept his children?

He had brought her here to his home in the hope that when she got to know them she would love them as he did. But today, of all days, they'd chosen to behave badly. Usually Antonio was protective of the smaller boys. He might tease them or tell them to get lost, but he never really fought with them. Carlitos, though he had a temper, had never before picked up anything from the table and thrown it. Even Lucita had behaved badly when he insisted she eat her vegetables before the ice cream.

He loved his children, but today he'd almost wished he did have an attic to lock them in.

But the truth, of course, was that he would never lock them away or put them away from him. They were his, he loved them, and he was committed to them. If Kristen couldn't accept them, then how could they have a future?

Tonight, after he and Kristen made love, he'd slept more soundly than usual. That was why he hadn't heard Gretyl cry out right away. By the time he grabbed a robe and ran down to her room, Kristen had already been there, holding Gretyl in her arms. He'd started in, then stopped. Kristen was handling it. He watched her stroke Gretyl's hair, and heard her sing in English, a song he'd never heard before, in a funny off-key voice.

Something had knotted in his throat, and he'd felt a flare of hope because maybe, after all, there was a chance for both him and his children.

Sunlight found its way into Kristen's room. She felt its warmth and snuggled her face into her goosedown pillow. It had taken her a long time to get back to sleep after Gretyl's nightmare, and now, in spite of the sun, she wanted to go back to sleep.

Someone knocked on her door. She struggled to open her eyes and mumbled, "Who is it?"

"Me."

"Who's me?"

"Lucita. May I come in?"

Kristen groaned, tempted to say, "Come back tomorrow." Instead, she muttered, "All right."

Lucita opened the door, then bent down and picked a tray up off the floor.

"I fixed your breakfast," she said.

"Oh." Kristen tried to rub the sleep out of her eyes. "That's nice."

The eight-year-old beamed. "All by myself." She brought the tray to the bed and put it across Kristen's legs. Then stood back expectantly.

There was burned toast smeared with peanut butter, a banana, a glass of milk and a piece of chocolate cake.

"My," Kristen said. "Doesn't this look..." She searched for the right word and settled on "Wonderful."

"Manuela said that maybe you'd rather have breakfast in the dining room, but I thought it would be nicer to have it in bed." She looked at the tray and then at Kristen. "Do you like it?"

Kristen took a bite of the burned toast. The peanut butter stuck to the roof of her mouth. She sipped the cold milk and said, "The toast is delicious. Would you like a piece?"

"Okay." Lucita grinned. "That's the only word I know in English, but maybe while you're here you could teach me some more words."

"Okay," Kristen said, and that made Lucita laugh.

She said, "Thank you for the blouse. I put it on so you could see it. I like the headband, too." She crawled on the bed beside Kristen and reached for a piece of toast. "This is better than eating with everybody," she said. "Is it all right if I have a drink of your milk?"

"Of course."

"Do you like it here?"

"Yes, I do. It's a beautiful house."

"But the boys are noisy, aren't they?"

"Maybe a little."

Lucita sighed. "I guess that's just the way boys are."

"Probably."

"Did Gretyl have a nightmare last night?"

"Yes, she did. I hope she didn't wake you."

"No, it's all right. I woke up for a minute, but then I went back to sleep." Lucita took another bite of toast. "She has lots of bad dreams, and sometimes she's real sad. I guess because she misses her mother and father. They got killed, like my mother and father did." She looked up at Kristen. "Do you have a mother?"

"No, my parents died, too."

Lucita patted her hand. "That's too bad," she said. "I'm really sorry."

The breath caught in Kristen's throat and she felt tears spring to her eyes.

"Eat some cake." Lucita took a bite. "It'll make you feel better."

Kristen hugged her. "*You* make me feel better," she said. "Okay, let's both eat the cake."

"For breakfast?" Fernando asked from the doorway.

Lucita, her mouth rimmed with chocolate, looked up at him. "I brought the Señorita Kristen her breakfast," she said.

"That was thoughtful of you, sweetheart. But maybe she'd like something else. Manuela is fixing pecan waffles."

"Pecan waffles?"

"And maybe Kristen would like to get dressed." He picked Lucita up off the bed and kissed her chocolaty mouth. "Go wash your face, and then tell Manuela that Señorita Kristen and I will be there in ten minutes."

"Sure." She looked back at Kristen. "You'll come pretty soon, yes?"

"Yes, I'll come, but the breakfast you fixed is so good, I don't think I can eat another bite."

"We could divide the waffle like we did the cake."
Lucita smiled. "Hurry up, though, okay?"

"Okay." Kristen said with a laugh. And when the
little girl went skipping down the hallway, she said,
"She's cute as a button."

"So are you." He took the tray away, then leaned
to lick a smudge of chocolate off her mouth. "Um,
that's good," he said, and kissed her.

"I've got to get up," she murmured against his lips.

"In a minute."

"The door's open. The children might see."

"See me kissing you? I don't think they'd be too
surprised." He brushed the tangled hair back from her
face. "I certainly like the way you look in the morning, Señorita Fielding. It takes my breath away." He
cupped her face between his hands. "Have I told you
how wonderful last night was? How much it meant to
me?"

Color crept into her cheeks. "Me too," she whispered. "But we shouldn't have. The children—"

"Were safely tucked in their beds at the other end
of the house. We were alone, the door was locked, and
you were irresistible."

"So were you." She kissed him, took a quick nip of
his earlobe and said, "Now get out of here and let me
get dressed."

He sighed, then, with a grin, said, "There's always
tonight."

"Out!" She pointed at the door. "Right now."

"I'm *loco* for you, Señorita Fielding."

"Just *loco*," she said. "Just *loco*."

* * *

They all spent the afternoon on the beach. "They're going to start tearing down some of those old piers next week," Fernando told Kristen. "It's liable to be noisy when they do, so we'd better get some beach time in while we can."

While the other boys played in the surf and Lucita and Gretyl, along with Kristen, built a sand castle, Fernando tried to teach four-year-old Hassan how to swim.

"Don't let go! Don't let go!" the little boy cried every time he thought Fernando might.

"I won't," Fernando assured him over and over again.

"Let me have him for a while." Antonio swam up beside them. "I'll be careful of him, *Tío*. Don't worry, I'm a good swimmer. I won't let anything—" He stopped. His expression changed.

"What is it?"

Antonio pointed down the beach, and Fernando turned to see a man staggering toward them. His clothes were rumpled and dirty. He wore a soiled red bandanna around his head. When he came closer, Fernando saw that he had a three-day growth of beard, and that he looked vaguely familiar.

"Don't worry," he assured Antonio. "He won't bother us."

"*¡Hola!*" the man called out. "Antonio! *¿Como estas?*"

"Do you know him?"

"He's . . . he's my uncle Casimiro."

"Your uncle?" Fernando remembered then where he'd seen the Gypsy. In the bar in Granada. The man had been drunk; he'd struck Antonio. He was drunk now, too.

"Go play with the other boys, Hassan," he said, and with his hand on Antonio's shoulder waited for the man to approach.

"Antonio." The Gypsy reached for the boy, staggered, then righted himself, embraced Antonio, and with his hand around his shoulders said, "I've come to take you with me."

The color drained out of Antonio's face. "Take me—?" He tried to move away, but the grip on his shoulders tightened.

"You don't belong here with fancy folks, you belong with us, with me. I've been trying to find you for months. Took me damn long enough. The whole camp's moving on to Sevilla, and you're coming with us. The April fair." He laughed. "Lots of easy pickin's, boy, so get your stuff together and let's go."

"Antonio's not going anywhere," Fernando said.

"He's my *pariente,* my kin. He should be back where he belongs and start earning his keep."

"Antonio is my son," Fernando said. "I've adopted him legally, and there's nothing you can do about it."

"*Your* son!" Hands on his hips in a threatening stance, Casimiro glared at Fernando.

"Kristen." Fernando didn't turn. "Take the children into the house, please."

"Yes, all right." She hesitated and then in English, said, "Should I call the police?"

"No, I can handle it."

He heard her murmur to the children, heard their questioning voices, and her reply, "Come along now, we're going in."

"All those kids yours?" Casimiro asked.

"Yes, they're my children."

"Then you don't need Antonio."

"You're not welcome here," Fernando said, ignoring the remark. "I want you to leave."

"You going to make me? Casimiro laughed and, stepping closer to Fernando, said, "I know all about you, rich lawyer. You think you're better'n me, don't you? I tell you what—you like the kid so much, you can keep him. You pay me, and maybe I go away."

Of course. He should have known. Casimiro's pretending he had come to take Tonio was only a ruse; he didn't want the boy, he wanted money. He glared at the Gypsy. "Get the hell out of here!" he said.

The uncle shook his head. "Twenty thousand pesetas and I go away for a while."

Without taking his eyes from the other man, Fernando said, "Antonio, go in the house and call the police."

"But I—" The ten-year-old swallowed hard. *"Muy bien, Tío,"* he said, and started toward the house.

"Come back here!" Casimiro roared.

"Go on, son." Fernando looked toward the boy to make sure he'd reached the house.

"Tío Nando!" Antonio screamed. "Watch out."

Fernando whirled around, saw the knife, made a grab for Casimiro's wrist, and felt the hot sting of the blade slashing into his arm. He got the other man's wrist with both hands, but the Gypsy was strong as a bull. He struck Fernando in the face. Fernando tightened his grip and twisted to try to make the Gypsy drop the knife. Casimiro grunted, dug his feet into the sand and struggled to hold onto it.

Blood ran down Fernando's arm, but still he hung on, twisting as hard as he could until the knife dropped. When it did, he shot a blow to the Gypsy's stomach. The man doubled over on the sand, but came up screaming and flung a handful of sand in Fernando's face.

For a moment, Fernando was blinded, unable to see. Casimiro gave him a blow to the face, and one to the side of the head that staggered him. Fernando struck out, connected with two fast blows to Casimiro's face, another to his midsection. Casimiro screamed in rage and came at Fernando, giant arms reaching out as though to crush him, leaving himself open and vulnerable.

Fernando hit him with his doubled-up fist, once, twice, fast, hard. The Gypsy faltered, but still he came on. Fernando sparred, then, with every bit of his strength, struck a blow to Casimiro's throat with the hard side of his hand.

Casimiro went to his knees, clutching his throat, beaten, unable to move. Blood ran down Fernando's arm. He stood, spread-legged to keep his balance, and tried to fight a wave of dizzyness.

"Tío!" Antonio cried. *"¡Tío,* you're bleeding!"

"No...no es nada," Fernando managed to say.

"Fernando!"

As though from a distance, he heard Kristen's voice. He looked toward her. She seemed to shimmer in the light. He said, "Maybe...maybe you'd better call the police."

"I already did. They're on their way, and so is an ambulance."

"He doesn't need an ambulance," he said, nodding toward Casimiro.

"No, but you do."

He looked at his bloody arm. "No *es una problema.*"

"No problem!" Tears stood in her eyes. His arm was cut from the shoulder almost to the elbow. She took off the scarf she'd put on to cover her hair earlier and wrapped it around his arm.

They heard the sirens, and a moment later Adela called out from the house, "The police are here, Señor Ibarra, and so is the ambulance."

Three policemen ran around the side of the house, followed by two paramedics carrying a stretcher.

"Here's the man," Fernando said to the police. "Lock him up for a couple of days and send him on his way."

One of the policemen hauled Casimiro to his feet. The man mumbled, *"¡Cabrones! ¡Todos cabrones!"*

"You don't want to file charges, *licenciado?*" one of the other policemen asked.

"All I want to do is get him out of town and make sure he doesn't bother me again."

"You'd better let me take care of that arm, sir." One of the paramedics started to unwrap Kristen's blood-soaked scarf, and when he did, he whistled and said, "That's some kind of a wound."

"Just needs a bandage," Fernando said.

"No, sir, it needs stitching. If you'll just lie down on the stretcher, we'll—"

"I can walk." He looked at Antonio. The boy was pale, his mouth was quivering. He put his good arm around Antonio's shoulders and said, "I'm all right, son. You go on in the house now."

"¿Tío—?"

"You're the oldest. The other children are probably frightened. I'm counting on you to tell them everything is all right."

Antonio bit his lip. Then, with a nod and a last look at Fernando, he turned and ran back to the house.

A paramedic put a pressure pack on Fernando's arm and quickly wrapped it. "That'll hold until we get to the hospital," he said.

Kristen put her arm around his waist. "I'm coming with you," she said.

"You don't have to do that."

"Yes, I do."

A paramedic took Fernando's good arm and led him around the house to the ambulance, which waited next to the police car. The officers put Casimiro into the backseat, and Fernando said, "Just a minute," to the paramedics.

He went to the police car. He was staggering now, and his face was very white. "Don't come back," he told the Gypsy. "If you try to take Antonio, I'll see to it that you spend one hell of a long time in jail. I'm his legal parent, and there's not a damn thing you can do about it."

Casimiro mumbled a string of obscenities. One of the officers said, "Shut up!" and he did.

The two paramedics helped Fernando into the ambulance and onto a cot. He closed his eyes and reached for Kristen's hand. "The children..." He took a deep breath to try to clear his head. "They'll be frightened."

"Adela and Manuela are with them."

"You," he said. "You need to be there."

"But I ..." She hesitated. "Yes, all right, Fernando. I'll go back to the house as soon as I know you're all right."

"*Gracias,* Kristen. Knew I...I could count on you."

Count on her? To handle six frightened children? She swallowed hard. *"No problema,"* she said, mocking him.

The siren wailed. She looked at his white face and at the bandage on his arm, which was already soaked with blood. "It's going to be all right, Fernando," she told him.

"Sure." He didn't open his eyes. "He wanted to take Antonio. Wouldn't let him."

"Of course not."

One of the paramedics hooked up an IV. The other one took Fernando's blood pressure. "We'll be at the hospital in a few minutes," he said. "Don't worry about anything, sir. We're going to take good care of you. Your wife is right here with you."

"Wife," Fernando said. Then the light faded, and as though from a distance, he heard one of them say, "He's unconscious. Hurry, man. Hurry!"

Chapter Eleven

Fernando had been only semiconscious when they reached the hospital in Málaga and rushed him into the emergency room. Kristen, almost as pale as he had been when they wheeled him in, waited outside, pacing the hall for almost forty-five minutes before a doctor came out.

"We've stitched up Señor Ibarra's arm," he said. "He's going to be all right, but it was a nasty wound, and he lost a lot of blood. I think we'd better keep him here for a day or two. He's in his room now, if you'd like to see him."

She thanked the doctor and on wobbly legs made her way down a labyrinth of halls to the room where Fernando had been taken. His arm was bandaged, and there was an IV in his other arm.

He looked up when she came in. "You look worse

than I do," he said, and gave her a lopsided smile.

"How...how do you feel?"

"A little groggy."

"You lost a lot of blood."

"Feels like a couple of quarts. That man, the uncle, he wanted to take Antonio. I couldn't let him."

"Of course not."

"When I said I wouldn't give him up, he tried to sell him to me."

"Sell him? My God!"

"The night I first saw Antonio, the night in Granada when his uncle hit him...when I took him to the hospital, there were marks on his back where that *cabron* Casimiro had beaten him. He may still try to get him..."

His voice weakened, failed. Kristen moved to his side. "Don't think about it now. The police took him away. He can't hurt Antonio anymore."

"Afraid...afraid he'll come back...try to take Tonio." Fernando opened his eyes and tried to sit up. "Be careful, Kristen. Keep Antonio in the house."

"I will." She eased him back against the pillows. "You've lost a lot of blood," she said. "You're weak. You've got to rest. I'll be right here."

"Time? What...what time is it?"

"A little after six."

"You'd better go."

She reached for his hand. "I want to stay with you."

"Kristen..." It was hard to concentrate. He was tired, half out of it. "The children..." he managed to say. "They probably saw what happened. If they saw Casimiro stab me, they're probably scared out of their wits. They need to know I'm all right. You tell them."

"I'll phone the house."

"No." He rested for a moment. "I need you to tell them I'm all right. To take care of them."

"I'll call Adela. Tell her—"

"No. You. Better you."

But I'm almost a stranger, she wanted to say. I don't know them that well, and they don't know me. How do I assure six very frightened children that, though their father is in the hospital, he's going to be all right? Adela knew them better than she did, she took care of them, stayed with them when Fernando was away. She was kind and efficient, a no-nonsense woman. But was efficiency what the children needed tonight?

Antonio might blame himself because Fernando had been hurt. Carlitos and Lucita would be afraid they had lost the uncle who had cared for them since their parents' death. Hassan and Ahmed were probably still terrified. And Gretyl. How frightened she must be.

As frightened as she herself had been.

Fernando lay with his eyes closed, his face pale, the bandaged arm at his side. What if he hadn't thrown his arm up? What if the Gypsy had found his true mark? She leaned her head against Fernando's side, needing to feel his warmth, to hear his breathing.

He touched the top of her head. "I'm sorry... About all this, I mean," he said. "Leaving you to look after the children. I wanted us to have a good time together. I'm... I'm so sorry this happened, Kristen."

"Oh, no." She sat up. "Oh, darling, no. All that matters is that you're all right."

"Señorita?" A man in the uniform of the Guardia Civil, the civil police, stood in the open doorway.

"May I come in?" he asked. "If Señor Ibarra is able, I would like to speak to him for a few moments."

"Come in," Fernando said.

"Ah, Señor Ibarra. I am sorry to disturb you, but if you feel well enough, I would like to ask you a few questions."

Kristen got up, and the officer moved closer to the bed. "The man who stabbed you, Casimiro Fuentes, is in jail. If I understand correctly from the officers, he attacked you when you were on the beach with the children and attempted to take the oldest boy away. Is that correct?"

Fernando nodded.

"You told the police you did not want to file charges, but I'm not sure that's wise. Our department has checked with the Guardia in Granada. The man Fuentes has a record of violence, and he's been locked up before. I'm afraid if we release him he'll try to get at you again, or to the boy he claims is his nephew."

"Antonio is his nephew, all right," Fernando said. "But I'm the boy's legal parent, and there's not a damn thing Casimiro about it."

"Still, in my opinion, you should press charges. The man assaulted you."

"He tried to kill you." Kristen shuddered. "I think you should do what the officer says, Fernando. What if he comes back?"

"He was on his way to the Sevilla fair before this happened. Once he's let out of jail, he'll join the rest of the group and head there."

"Perhaps," the policeman said. "Perhaps not."

Fernando leaned back against his pillow, suddenly too exhausted to argue. "No charges," he insisted.

"Just . . . keep him locked up for four or five days. Warn him that if he bothers me again or tries to get to Antonio, I'll press charges for attempted murder." He looked up at Kristen. "He's Tonio's uncle," he explained. "It would hurt the boy to know his uncle was in prison because of me."

"But—" She bit back the words, because she knew this wasn't the time to argue with Fernando. He had to rest and get his strength back. They could talk about it again, but not now.

"You need to rest," she said, and to the officer she added, "I'm sure Señor Ibarra will feel more like talking tomorrow. Perhaps you could come back then."

"Very well." The man shook his head. "But I think you're making a mistake, *señor*."

"Perhaps." Then, "Señorita Fielding is going back to Santa Cruz de la Palma. Would you be kind enough to see her to a taxi?"

"I myself will drive her, Señor Ibarra."

"*Gracias.*" Fernando took Kristen's hand. "You go with the officer," he said. "I'm all right. Tell the children."

"I will." She stepped closer and, leaning down, brushed a kiss across his lips. "I don't want to leave you," she whispered.

"I know."

"I'll be back in the morning."

"Have Enrique drive you." He squeezed her hand. "Go with the officer, Kristen. Tell the children I'll be home soon." He hesitated for a moment. "When I'm there, they like me to tuck them in and say good-night. If you wouldn't mind . . ."

"I wouldn't mind."

She didn't want to leave him. She wanted to stay here in the room with him, to sit in a chair beside the bed, so that she could touch him. But there were the children to think of. She had to do what Fernando asked.

At the door, she looked back. He smiled, she smiled back. Then, quickly, before she could change her mind, followed the officer out of the room.

"It's my fault," Antonio said.

"No, it isn't." They were gathered together in the living room, Kristen on one of the sofas, the children around her.

"If I'd gone with my uncle Tío Nando wouldn't have gotten hurt."

"It would have hurt him a lot more than he's hurt now if he'd lost you." She took his hand and drew him close. "You're his son, and he loves you. He'd never let anyone take you away from him."

"Is—is he going to die?" Carlito's chin trembled, and he started to cry.

"Of course not." She pulled the five-year-old up onto her lap. "He has to stay in the hospital for another day or two, that's all. The doctors and nurses are taking good care of him."

"Could we call him up on the telephone?" Lucita asked.

"Maybe tomorrow. Tonight he has to rest and go to sleep."

"What if he got killed?" Hassan wanted to know. "What if that man comes back and kills him until he's dead?"

"What would happen to us then?" Ahmed's dark eyes were wide and frightened. "Would we have to go back to Tangier?"

"Well, first of all, Tío Nando didn't get killed," Kristen said. "And second of all, you'll never have to go back to Tangier, neither you nor Hassan. This is your home, and you belong here."

"Are you going to stay until Tío Nando comes back?" Lucita asked.

"Of course I am," Kristen assured her. She looked at Gretyl, who, silent as a frightened mouse, sat on a footstool, as close to her as she could get. She rested a hand on Gretyl's head and said, "Tío Nando is going to be all right. He'll be home with us in two or three days. Meantime, I'm right here, and I'm not going anywhere."

Gretyl looked up at her. "Not ever?" she whispered.

"Well . . ." Kristen hesitated. "Well, of course, I'll have to go back to New York, because that's where I live. But not right away. Certainly not until Tío Nando returns and we all know that he's well and strong again."

Gretyl bowed her head, and she didn't move again until Adela came to say that dinner was ready.

As soon as she got home, both Adela and Manuela had appeared to ask about Fernando. When Kristen assured them that he was going to be all right, Manuela had said, "I haven't started dinner, Señorita. I was waiting until I heard how Señor Ibarra was before I fixed anything."

"Then how about something simple? Hamburgers and French fries?"

Manuela smiled. "The children would love that. We only have hamburgers on special occasions."

"I think this is a special occasion."

"I made a chocolate cake."

"Good," Kristen said. "We'll have that for dessert, along with ice cream."

When the children were seated around the dining room table, Kristen said, "We're having hamburgers tonight."

"With French-fried potatoes?" Ahmed asked. "I love French-fried potatoes."

Carlitos tried to blink the tears out of his eyes. "Me too."

As soon as Carmelita served them, he reached across the table and took one.

Lucita said, "You're not supposed to reach. You're supposed to say, "Please pass me the French-fried potatoes."

"Stop being so prissy," Antonio said.

"I'm not prissy!"

"Yes, you are."

"Don't say bad things to my sister," Carlitos said.

"He's always picking on me." Lucita's chin wobbled.

"That's because you're a girl," Ahmed said.

"No, it's not. I—"

"That's quite enough," Kristen said, in the same authoritative tone she often used at board meetings.

All six of the children looked at her, too surprised to say anything.

"There will be no more bickering at the table. Is that understood?"

Eyes wide, they nodded.

"Lucita, pass your brother the potatoes. Hassan, use both hands when you pick up your milk. Ahmed, wipe your mouth with your napkin, not the back of your hand."

They all sat up straighter. Antonio looked surprised, the younger children a little awed.

Well, Kristen thought with a sense of triumph, this is easier than I'd expected it to be. I'll just pretend I'm in the boardroom—be serious enough to snap 'em to and get their attention, then smile.

Which was exactly what she did when she said, with a smile, "There's chocolate cake and ice cream for dessert."

They smiled back, a little uncertainly, and Lucita said, "Could we watch a movie after?"

"Of course," Kristen said. "What would you like to see?"

"We've got *Aladdin*," Carlitos said. "I like that."

"You've already seen it about twenty times." Antonio shook his head. "What about *Batman?*"

"That scares me," Lucita said.

"Me too," Hassan put in.

"I like it," Ahmed said.

"We'll put it to a vote," Kristen decided, back in the boardroom once again. "The majority will decide."

They looked astounded.

"All in favor of seeing *Aladdin* raise your hands."

Carlitos, Hassan, Lucita and Gretyl raised their hands.

"*Batman?*"

Only Antonio and Ahmed raised their hands.

"*Aladdin* it is," Kristen said, smiling like a benevolent judge.

They watched the film in what Adela said was the patio room. There was a sofa there, as well as comfortable chairs and a twenty-six-inch television set. Lucita sat on one side of Kristen on the sofa, four-year-old Hassan on the other side. They all enjoyed the movie, even Antonio, and when it was over Kristen said, "Time for bed."

"Maybe we could have some more ice cream," Carlitos said.

"No," Kristen firmly. "It's bedtime."

"Will you come tuck us in?" Lucita asked.

"There's no need to bother the Señorita Kristen," Adela said from the doorway. "I'll come in later."

"It's no bother," Kristin said. "Thank you, Adela, but I'll say good-night to the children."

"Well..." The housekeeper looked surprised. "If you want to."

"I want to."

Twenty minutes later, she went to the room Hassan and Ahmed shared. They were in their beds; Hassan, his thumb in his mouth, was already half-asleep. She pulled the light blanket up over his shoulders and kissed his cheek. Then Ahmed's. *"Buenas noches, niños,"* she said. "Sleep well."

Next was Carlitos's and Antonio's room. Carlitos was already asleep, but Antonio wasn't. His eyes were red; he turned away.

Kristen sat on the side of his bed. "What is it?" she asked. "Are you worried about Fernando?"

He nodded. "It's my fault he got hurt. What if he dies? What if—?"

"Shh," she said. "He's not going to die, Tonio. And I told you before, it wasn't your fault."

"It was Uncle Casimiro who hurt him. That makes it my fault."

"No, it doesn't."

"What if he comes back?"

"He won't. He's in jail now, and when he gets out he's going to Sevilla."

"To pick pockets." Antonio buried his head in his pillow.

"But that doesn't have anything to do with you. You don't belong to your uncle, you're Fernando's son. He loves you very much, and he always will."

She rubbed his back. "I'm going to the hospital in the morning. I can't take any of the other children, because they're too young, but I'll take you, so that you can see for yourself that Tío Nando is all right. Would you like that?"

He turned to look up at her. "Would you really take me with you?"

"Of course." She kissed his forehead. "Go to sleep now, Tonio."

"All right." He swallowed hard. "I'm glad you're here, Señorita Kristen. I hope you stay for a long time."

She smiled. But all she said was "Good night, Antonio. Sleep well."

Lucita and Gretyl were next. When she went into their room, Lucita said, "Is Tío really all right?"

"Yes, he is. He'll be home in a few days, and you can see for yourself." She kissed Lucita's cheek. "Now close your eyes and go to sleep."

She moved to the other bed. "You too, Gretyl. It's way past your bedtime."

The little girl clutched her teddy bear. "Will you still be here when we wake up?"

"Of course I will." She pulled the blanket up over Gretyl's shoulders. "Good night," she said. "You too, Otto." That brought a small smile, so she kissed Gretyl's cheek as she had Lucita's.

"*Gracias,* Señorita Krissy."

"Señorita Krissy?" It was Kristen's turn to smile. "I think I like that. Good night, girls. Sleep well."

"Good night, Señorita Krissy," they said in unison. Lucita giggled, but Gretyl didn't. She only looked at Kristen, her blue eyes so serious. So sad.

The next morning, true to her word and over the protests of the five other children, all of whom wanted to go, too, Kristen took Antonio with her to Málaga. She had phoned the hospital last night, before she went to bed and again this morning. Señor Ibarra was resting well, she'd been told. There really was no need to worry.

But she did worry, of course. Finally, after an almost sleepless night, she got up, showered, drank coffee and waited for the children to get up and have their breakfast. As soon as they did, she and Antonio left for the hospital with Enrique.

"But the boy is only ten," a nurse on Fernando's floor said when she saw Antonio."

"I know." Kristen put her hand on Antonio's shoulder. "He'll only stay for a few minutes, and then he'll be driven home. It's very important that he see Señor Ibarra. Please let him stay."

"Very well," the nurse said reluctantly. "Señor Ibarra is much better. The doctor saw him earlier, and will see him again in a little while. If he continues to do well, I should think he'd be able to go home tomorrow.''

''Tomorrow?'' Antonio looked relieved. ''Really?''

''You see?'' Kristen said. ''I told you he was going to be all right.''

She took his hand then, and together they went down the hall to Fernando's room. The IV was still connected, but he looked a hundred times better than he had yesterday afternoon.

''Good morning,'' Kristen said from the doorway. ''Look who's come to visit you.''

''Antonio.'' Fernando smiled. ''What a nice surprise.''

The boy stood in the doorway until Kristen said, ''It's all right, Tonio. You can go in.''

''Come give me *un abrazo,*'' Fernando said. The boy leaned down to embrace him, so awkwardly, so carefully, that Fernando laughed. ''It's all right, Tonio, I won't break.''

''Are you better?''

''Yes, *muchacho,* I'm much better.''

He looked better, Kristen thought. There was more color in his face, and his voice was stronger.

''The nurse at the desk said Antonio could only stay a few minutes,'' she said. ''Hospital rules. I thought I'd try to find a cup of coffee and let the two of you visit for a little while.''

''All right, but I'd like *un abrazo* from you, too.''

She gave him a gentle hug. ''My pleasure, Señor Ibarra,'' she said.

"And mine." He smiled up at her. "No trouble with the children?"

"No, they were fine—but worried about you, of course."

"What about dinner? Much of a hassle?"

"Why, no. I just pretended that I was in the board-room and that I was the one running the meeting." She grinned. "It worked."

He laughed, and when Kristen stood and started for the door, he motioned Antonio forward and said, "Come and sit beside me, Tonio."

She left them alone then, and when she returned twenty minutes later, they were both smiling.

"That nurse came in," Antonio said. "She told me I had to leave, and I said I couldn't until my *tía* came back."

His *aunt?* She wasn't sure how she felt about that. She'd only been in Fernando's house for three days. It wasn't a good idea for the children to become attached to her so quickly. She had promised Fernando she would stay for two weeks; now she wondered if that had been a mistake.

Fernando looked up at her. "Aunt Kristen," he said in English. "How does that sound?"

"A little strange," she said uncertainly.

The nurse Kristen had seen earlier stuck her head in the door. "It's time, young man," she announced.

"Can't I stay, *Tío?*"

"I'm afraid not. But I'll be home tomorrow. Until then, you do what—" Fernando hesitated and with a grin said, "Whatever Tía Kristen tells you to do. And remember, you're older than the other children. It's up to you to set a good example."

"I will." He leaned down and gave Fernando a careful hug, and to Kristen he said, "You don't have to come with me. I know where Enrique's parked."

"But I want to." And to Fernando she said, "I'll be right back."

She took Antonio to the car, gave him a hug and said, "Take care of the others."

"I will, *Tía*."

Tía. Darn, she thought. This is getting too close for comfort.

But when she went back to Fernando, she didn't say anything about Antonio's calling her "aunt." Instead, she told him about the other children, about their dinner of hamburgers and French fries, and that later they had all watched *Aladdin* together.

She stayed with Fernando until late afternoon. The doctor came while she was there. He checked Fernando's vital signs, looked at his arm and said, "You're coming along. Perhaps you can go home tomorrow, if you promise to take it easy for a few days.

"I promise."

"No lifting. I know you've got children, but you're not to pick them up." The doctor, a grizzled older man with a long and solemn face, turned to Kristen. "You be sure he doesn't."

"I will."

"All right. I'll see you in the morning, Señor Ibarra. If you're still doing as well as you are now I'll release you. Your *novia*, your fiancée, can pick you up."

A little while ago she'd become an aunt. Yesterday she'd been a wife, and now she was a fiancée. Things were going so fast she wanted to say, "Hey, wait a minute."

And, as though reading her thoughts, Fernando looked at her, his expression questioning. But he didn't say anything, and in a little while he dozed off.

But still Kristen sat there beside him, holding his hand, while the words *novia*, *tía* and *wife* ran around and around in her head.

Chapter Twelve

Fernando wasn't a very good patient. It wasn't that he complained or asked to be waited on. The problem was that he ignored the fact that he'd been hurt and needed a few days to recuperate. He insisted on doing everything for himself, and if he grimaced in pain because he moved too quickly, he covered the pain with a joke or a shrug.

Kristen tried not to hover over him, but it was hard not to. His fight with the Gypsy, the knife wound and his being carried away in the ambulance had frightened the life out of her. If she hadn't known before how much she cared for Fernando, she knew it now. When the Gypsy's knife cut into his arm, his pain had become her pain.

The day he returned from the hospital, she insisted

that he go right to bed, and succeeded in keeping him there that day and most of the next.

For the next few days, without being really aware of it, she began to take over the supervision of the household and the children. She consulted with Manuela over the week's menu. She drove Lucita to her ballet class and Gretyl to her appointment with the child psychologist in Málaga. She fished off the pier with Antonio and gave swimming lessons to Hassan and Ahmed. Cute little boys with big black eyes and infectious smiles, they romped through the water, laughing, splashing each other and her. And when four-year-old Hassan wound his arms around her neck and said, "Hang on to me, Tía Krissy, hang on," she experienced a softening flutter of warmth.

Because Fernando rested a good deal those first few days after he returned from the hospital, the children turned more and more to her when they had a question or a need. And though Gretyl rarely spoke, she followed Kristen wherever she went, a silent but constant shadow.

That worried Kristen most of all.

She had agreed to stay for two weeks, and now the two weeks had become three. But how could she leave Fernando, when he was hurt? How could she leave the children, when they needed her? She would stay another week, she told herself. By then Fernando would be all right and the children would once more feel secure.

He went to his office several mornings, but the afternoons were spent on the beach with Kristen and the children. Workmen had started tearing down the old piers farther down, but so far the noise hadn't been enough to bother them.

As Fernando watched Kristen with his children, he thought about what it would be like if she was his wife. Of how it would be at the end of the day, when the children were safely in their beds and he and Kristen were alone.

They hadn't made love since that night in his study, and today, as he watched her, he felt his body grow hard with need. Maybe it was all the rest he'd been getting, or the rare steaks she had Manuela prepare for him, or maybe it was the sea air. Whatever it was the sight of her in the skimpy bikini, tall and tanned and blond, turned him on as nothing ever had.

When she brought Hassan and Ahmed out of the water and made sure they were occupied looking for seashells, she ran over to Fernando.

"Are you feeling all right?" she asked. "Can I get you anything? Does your arm hurt?"

"Not my arm," he said.

She looked anxious. "Is something wrong? Don't you feel well?"

"I feel very well. Too well." He grasped her ankle. "So well I'm about to burst with it."

A look of awareness cross her face, and she said, "Oh, my."

"Oh, my, indeed."

"It's too soon. You've been hurt."

"Only my arm, not the rest of me."

"This bears thinking about."

"It certainly does."

"We could talk about it."

"Talk wasn't what I had in mind."

She grinned, but at that moment they heard Carlitos roar, "You stepped on my castle!" and with a cry of rage he punched Ahmed.

Fernando started up out of his chair, but Kristen said, "No, stay where you are. I'll handle it."

She ran over to the boys, separated them, told Carlitos that he was not to hit Ahmed or anyone else. "Hands aren't for hitting," Fernando heard her say. "Now behave yourself."

"He stepped on my castle."

"He didn't mean to. Anyway, you can build a new castle tomorrow. Right now, it's time for all of you to go in and have your baths before dinner."

"I'll help Tío Nando." Antonio ran to Fernando, and though Fernando was perfectly capable of getting up by himself, he let the boy take his arm and help him up out of the beach chair.

Like Kristen, Antonio had hovered over Fernando ever since he'd returned from the hospital. "Are you all right?" he asked twenty times a day. "Does your arm hurt?"

And though Fernando grew impatient with the constant questions, he always said, because he knew Antonio still blamed himself for the stabbing, "I'm fine, Tonio."

This morning the police had called to say they were going to release Casimiro, with the warning that he leave the area and not return. He hoped Casimiro obeyed the warning. He hadn't pressed charges, because of Antonio, but if Casimiro showed his face again, he wouldn't hesitate.

The routine of his household hadn't changed during his brief stay in the hospital, yet there was a subtle difference in the children that he couldn't quite put his finger on. Lucita still chattered and giggled, Ahmed and Hassan still gave each other an occasional poke, but there was less bickering than before when they all sat down to lunch and dinner.

They called Kristen *Tía* or Krissy and vied for her attention. They told her made-up jokes and went to her to settle their arguments. And Gretyl, who watched Kristen with adoring eyes, got as close to her as she could, whenever she could. While Fernando was glad his children had adjusted so quickly to Kristen, it worried him, too. She was becoming a part of their lives; how would they feel when and if she left? Especially Gretyl. What would happen to Gretyl if Kristen left them?

On his first night home, the children, along with Kristen, had gone to his room to tell him good-night. One after the other they'd come to his bed and kissed his cheek, even shy little Gretyl. And when they'd said their final good-nights and turned to follow Kristen out of the room, Gretyl had reached for Kristen's hand and rubbed her face against it.

The gesture both touched and worried him.

As soon as he was able, he'd gone to the children's rooms to tell them good-night and tuck them in. "Come with me," he'd said to Kristen when he did.

"I have to phone the office," she said.

When she said the same thing the following night, he'd said, "The children miss your telling them good-night. Especially Lucita and Gretyl."

So she went with him, first to the boys' rooms, then to Lucita and Gretyl's room. She pulled the blankets up over the little girls and gently kissed both scrubbed little faces.

"Goodnight Tía Krissy," they said in unison.

"They made that up while you were in the hospital," she said. "I hope you don't mind."

"Of course not. Actually, it sounds rather nice." He linked his arm through hers. "How about a walk on the beach, Tía Krissy?" And when she hesitated, he said, "I need the exercise."

"All right. Thirty minutes, then you go to bed."

"You're worse than the nurses at the hospital." He took her arm as they started down the steps to the beach.

"I can't help it," she said. "I was so afraid. I still have bad dreams about him stabbing you." She clutched his good arm. "What if he comes back?"

"He won't. By tomorrow he'll be on his way to Sevilla."

"I hope so."

He put his arm around her waist. "It's over, *querida*. Besides, it's too nice a night to think about Casimiro."

It was a nice night, a still and beautiful night. The moon cast a silvery pattern on the water, the air smelled of the sea, and only the slightest of breezes rustled through the palms.

"It's so beautiful here." Kristen paused and stood looking out at the water. "I didn't want to come to Spain, you know. I had what I suppose was a mild breakdown, nothing serious, but I'd been working hard for a long time and I was exhausted." She hesitated for a moment, then decided to tell him the rest of it.

"There was a problem at the office," she said. "Someone I trusted, a woman I had brought into the company, had been stealing our formulas and selling them to a rival company. Not only that, she'd been having an affair with the man I had dated for two years."

A man. He didn't want to think about that. He put his arm around her. "I'm so sorry," he said.

"It doesn't seem to matter all that much now, but it did at the time. My doctor insisted I take a few weeks off. Tillie, my assistant and best friend, had been to Santa Cruz de la Palma the year before. She loved it here, and insisted I come."

"Remind me to thank her." He cupped Kristen's chin. "Stay here," he said. "Stay with me."

"Fernando, please. You know I have to go back to New York."

"Nothing is an absolute, Kristen."

"I need time."

"I need you."

"I own a business," she said. "I can't just turn and walk away from it."

"I don't expect you to. I know arrangements would have to be made, that it would take you a little time."

"A little time?" She shook her head. "You don't understand. It's my company. I'm proud of it, I like what I do, and I like my life the way it is."

"And there's no room in your life for me or my children?"

She searched for the words to tell him how she felt. "I care for you," she said. "I love being with you, and yes, I think I love you. But I'm not sure I'm cut out to be a wife and a mother. Perhaps in time..." She shook her head. "But not now. I don't think I can do it now."

"I see. You're asking for time, but you don't know how much time."

"No, I don't," she said, without meeting the intensity of his gaze.

In a little while, they started back to the house. When they reached it, she said, "I'm tired, Fernando. I think I'll go to bed now."

"Of course." He made no attempt to touch her. "Sleep well, Kristen. I'll see you in the morning."

She reached out to him. "I'm sorry," she said.

"Yes, so am I." As sorry as death, for surely losing her was a form of death.

She couldn't sleep. With all her heart, Kristen wanted to go to Fernando. She wanted to lie in his arms and tell him how sorry she was that she couldn't be the woman he wanted her to be. She wanted to say, "Maybe someday," but she knew that someday would never come.

Finally, restless but not wanting to take a sleeping pill, she got up and, throwing on a robe, went through the darkened corridors to the kitchen. Last night, Manuela had made a coconut cake. It would taste good with a glass of milk, and maybe the milk would help her sleep.

There was a dim light over the kitchen stove. She went barefoot across the floor to the refrigerator and peered inside. There were two pieces of cake on the plate. She took the plate out, then the milk, and, after she'd found a glass, a saucer and a fork, sat down at the kitchen table.

It felt a little strange, being here like this when everyone else was sleeping, but she needed the time alone. On Monday the children would go back to school. Perhaps it would be easier then, easier to leave when she knew they were back in a familiar routine.

She took a bite of the cake, a sip of the cold milk. And Fernando? Would it be easy to leave him?

Not in a lifetime. But how could she not? She couldn't stay in Spain. She had a company to run, people who depended on her. The children would miss her, and she would miss them, but children adapted. They'd miss her for a few days, and then they would forget.

And Fernando? Would he forget in time? Would he—?

She stopped, listening. Had one of the children called out? Perhaps Adela or Manuela had heard her stirring in the kitchen and gotten up to see who it was.

"Adela?" she said. "Manuela?"

There was no answer. She sat very still, and in a moment she heard it again, the sound of a footfall in the silence of the night.

"Who's there? Fernando, is that you?"

"No, *señorita,* it is I, Casimiro Fuentes."

The Gypsy stood in the open doorway of the kitchen. "Where is Señor Ibarra?" he whispered. "I would have a word with him."

Kristen's mouth went dry; she thought for a moment that she would faint. She took a deep breath and told herself she couldn't do that. She stood, not even aware she was still holding the glass of milk. "What are you doing here?"

"I have come to settle a small debt with the *señor*." He took a step toward her, brandishing an eight-inch knife.

She looked at it. She couldn't take her eyes off of it. "You will take me to him, yes?"

He took a step toward her. The glass of milk slipped from her fingers and fell with a crash. Casimiro muttered an oath. *"Estúpida!"* He looked down at the broken glass, the spilled milk. And when he did, unmindful of the glass, Kristen sprinted past him. She made it to the door before he grabbed her. She fought him, struck out with her fist and caught him a glancing blow on the side of his face. He hit her. She staggered back and stepped on pieces of the broken glass.

He grabbed her around the waist. "Take me to him!" he snarled. "Take me now, or I'll cut your throat before I cut his!"

She started to scream before he clapped a hand over her mouth. "Move," he whispered and, still holding her pushed her toward the door.

Fernando! His name screamed in her mind. He mustn't find Fernando!

The Gypsy shoved her out of the kitchen ahead of him. "Where are the bedrooms?" he whispered. "Take me there."

Her feet were cut, and she moaned in pain. The hand on her mouth tightened. "Go," he said. "Hurry."

They passed through the dining room and the living room, and into the dark corridor. The bedrooms lay ahead. Her mind raced. She could not, would not, lead him to Fernando's room. And the children. Dear God! She couldn't let him hurt the children. Her room, then. She'd take him to her room. And after that? She'd try to get away from him, scream for Fernando, fight him. But she would not lead him to Fernando.

She struggled to break free. He cursed and struck her on the side of her head with the back of the hand that held the knife. "You try it, I kill you, then I go to every room until I find him."

The children. Oh, God, the children.

The hand over her mouth was sweaty, and his breath smelled of sour wine. He held her with one hand around her waist, and she could feel the point of the knife against her back.

They were closer to the bedrooms. Hers was to the left, Fernando's to the right. Once they turned into the section of the corridor that held the bedrooms, there would be a hall light, but here the corridor was dark, the niches like ghostly hiding places where carved angels and silent saints stood on recessed pillars. Ahead she could see the dim light of the bedroom corridor.

"Which way?" he asked, his mouth close to her ear. "Nod your head."

She nodded to her left.

"*¡Andale!*" he whispered. "One move and . . ."

A figure leaped from one of the niches. The hand on her mouth loosened. The knife against her back fell. She heard the *whomp* of a blow. The Gypsy fell forward, taking her with him. She held her hands out to break the fall, then rolled hard toward the wall of the corridor and away from him.

She heard another *whomp* and put her fist against her mouth so that she wouldn't cry out.

"Kristen! Kristen, are you all right?"

"Y-yes," she managed to say. "Is he—is he dead?"

"No such luck." Fernando reached down a hand to help her up. "Get me a curtain cord," he said. "Something to tie him with."

She ran to her room, pulled at the cords that held the curtains and yanked them loose. When she went back to Fernando, he grabbed the Gypsy's hands and said, "Call the police while I tie him."

She went back to her room, got the operator and asked for the police. "We'll be there in ten minutes," the man who answered said.

Fernando came into her room. She said, "The police are coming." Then. "You're not wearing clothes."

He gripped her arms. "Did he hurt you? Are you all right?"

"Fine. I'm fine. I was in the kitchen. He came in. How did you—"

"Oh, my God," he said. "You're bleeding."

She looked down. There were bloody footprints across the floor. "I broke a glass," she said.

"Lie down. Let me look at your feet."

She shook her head. He was barefoot, wearing only his pajama bottoms. "The police are on the way," she said. "You'd better put a robe on."

"All right," he said. "Stay here."

But she couldn't. What if Antonio's uncle managed to free himself? What if he tried to hurt one of the children? She hobbled over to the dressing table, wrapped stockings around her feet, put on a pair of bedroom slippers, then a robe, and went out into the corridor, just as she heard the police sirens.

She opened the door and went into the girls' room, and when she saw that they were asleep, she went to

Ahmed's and Hassan's room. They, too, were sleeping. She went out and down the corridor to the room Carlitos and Antonio shared. Carlitos was asleep, but Antonio was sitting up in bed.

"What's happening?" He sounded frightened. "I heard something, like somebody fighting, and then I heard the sirens." He clutched at the sheet. "Is it Uncle Casimiro? Is he here?"

Kristen hesitated. From the corridor she heard someone say, "We'll take it from here, Señor Ibarra. You're going to press charges this time, aren't you?"

"You're damn right I am. I'll come down to headquarters first thing in the morning. By the time I get through with this *cabron,* he'll be in prison until he's tripping over his beard."

"What did you hit him with?"

"A saint from one of the niches."

Somebody laughed.

"When prayer doesn't work…" somebody else said.

"They're going to keep him in jail this time?" Antonio whispered.

"For a very long time." Kristen put her arms around him. "It's over, Tonio. You're safe."

"Sometimes…" His voice choked. "Sometimes I'm scared I'll have to go back. To Granada, I mean." He started to cry. "I don't want to go back. I'd die before I go back."

"You won't have to. Fernando is your father. He'll never let anyone take you away from him." She eased him back against his pillows.

He knuckled his tears away. "Don't tell the other kids that I was crying."

"I won't." She smoothed the dark hair back from his forehead. "Go to sleep now," she said. "I'll be right here."

He reached for her hand and held it, held it until, with a sigh, he closed his eyes and went to sleep.

Fernando found her there. "I told you to stay in your room."

"I was worried about the children." She looked down at the sleeping boy. "Tonio heard the commotion, he was frightened."

"Poor boy. But it's over now. As soon as Casimiro gets out of the hospital, he'll go to jail."

"You hit him that hard?"

"I wish I'd killed him." He scooped Kristen up in his arms and carried her out of the room. "When I saw him holding you like that, when I saw the knife against your back..." He buried his face against her hair and a shudder ran through him. "I woke up a few minutes after you left. I lay there thinking about you, about us, and then I heard something, like something breaking."

"I dropped a glass of milk."

He took her into her room and laid her on the bed. "I think I knew," he said. "Knew it was Casimiro, knew you were in trouble." He eased the slippers off her feet, then unwrapped the bloody stockings she'd wrapped around them. "I was afraid to come straight at him, afraid he'd hurt you, so I waited."

"And hit him."

"With poor Saint Cesareo." He picked her up off the bed and carried her into the bathroom.

The cut on the right foot was an inch long, the one on her left smaller but deeper. He washed both wounds with soap and water, put antiseptic cream on and bandaged them. When she winced, he said, "Sorry," and felt her pain as though it were his own.

When at last he carried her back to her bed, he lay down beside her. "I'm going to stay with you for what's left of the night," he said.

"But the children," Kristen protested.

"I'll tell them you were hurt."

"But—"

"Shh..." he said, and held her as she had held Antonio, until she, too, went to sleep.

Chapter Thirteen

Fernando held her through what was left of the night. And though he tried to sleep, each time he closed his eyes he heard the harsh whisper of Casimiro's voice and saw again the way the Gypsy had held her, his hand clamped over her mouth, the knife at her back. If anything had happened to Kristen . . . The thought sickened him. He tightened his arms around her. She moaned softly in her sleep, and when she snuggled closer and lay with her head in the hollow of his shoulder, he kissed the top of her head and held her with a love that went beyond passion, to the deepest caring he had ever known.

He left her when morning came and he knew it was time for the children to be up. He showered and dressed and, when he went back to her room, saw that she was still asleep. And that the children were up and clustered close to her door.

"What's the matter with Krissy?" Lucita asked. She stood with her hands on her hips, an anxious Gretyl right behind her. "How come she's still sleeping?"

Fernando hesitated. He didn't want to frighten them by telling them what had happened, but Antonio knew that Casimiro had been in the house last night and that the police had been here. He would be upset, and very possibly would tell the other children.

"The man I had a fight with on the beach came back last night," he said. "I called the police and they took him away. He won't be back again, I can promise you that."

"He was *here?*" Lucita's face paled. "In the house?"

"Yes, *querida,* but the police have him now, so we don't have to worry."

"But why is Krissy still asleep?" Gretyl whispered.

"She was awake when the police came, and before that..." And because he knew a small lie was called for here, he said, "She was in the kitchen having a glass of milk. She dropped the glass and cut her feet, so probably she's not going to feel like getting up for a while this morning." He put his arms around both girls. "We'll let her sleep. All right?"

They nodded solemnly and, holding hands, which they rarely did, tiptoed away with the boys.

He looked in on Kristen one more time, then closed her door and followed the children down the corridor.

* * *

She came awake slowly, not sure for a moment where she was. She remembered that last night she had been in Fernando's bed and that now she was here in her bed and that for a while he had been here with her. That brought a smile. She stretched a lazy cat stretch and gave a small yip of surprise, suddenly aware of the pain in both feet. The smile faded. She remembered Casimiro, her terror, the determination not to let him hurt Fernando again, and that terrifying moment when Fernando had leaped out of the darkness.

She looked at the clock. It was almost noon. She had to get up. Bathe, talk to Fernando.

A light knock on her door interrupted her thoughts, and she heard a small voice ask, "Krissy? Are you awake yet?"

"Yes, Lucita, I'm awake."

"Can we come in?"

"Of course."

The door opened, and the two little girls peeped in. "Are you all right?" Lucita asked, her face solemn, her voice hushed.

"Yes, *cielita linda,* I'm fine. Come in. You too, Gretyl."

Lucita came in, looked Kristen over for a moment, then crawled up on the bed next to her. "Tío Nando said that bad man was here last night."

"Yes, he was. The police took him away, and he isn't ever coming back."

"Did he hurt you?"

"No, I dropped a glass of milk, and then—" Kristen made a funny face. "And then I went and stepped on the broken glass."

Gretyl moved a little closer to the bed. "Did it hurt?"

"Yes, it did. But it's much better now." She patted the other side of the bed. "Why don't you come up here, so I can give both you and Lucita a good-morning hug?" And when Gretyl hesitated, Kristen said, "A hug for each foot. *Sí?*"

That brought the beginning of a smile. Gretyl came up onto the other side of the bed. Kristen put an arm around both little girls and hugged them. Then, with a laugh, she said, "It worked! My feet are better already."

Lucita giggled, and Gretyl smiled and said, "Really? Really, Krissy?"

"Really, sweetheart." She kissed Gretyl's nose, then Lucita's.

"We have to go back to school tomorrow," Lucita said. "And we don't get another vacation until all the way to summer."

"This is April," Kristen told her. "Vacation time is only two months away."

"I don't want to go to school," Gretyl said.

"But we have to go," Lucita said. "Pretty soon it will be summer, and then we can stay home with Krissy."

Tell them, Kristen thought. Tell both of them that you won't be here when summer comes. Tell them you have to leave.

She took a deep breath. "Girls, there's something I want to tell you. You know I live in New York."

"That was before," Lucita said. "Now you live here with us."

"Are you..." Gretyl's chin began to tremble. "Are you going away?"

"Not for a while," Fernando said from the door. And before either little girl could say anything, he added, "I bet Kristen is hungry. Why don't the two of you go tell Manuela to fix her a nice big breakfast?"

"But—" Lucita started to say.

"You can help," Fernando cut in. He picked each girl up off the bed, kissed their cheeks, and with a pat on each small fanny sent them out of the room.

"How do you feel?" he asked Kristen when they were alone.

"Fine, but I have to go to the bathroom."

"Let me help you."

"Let's see if I can navigate by myself first." She threw back the sheet, put her legs over the side of the bed and took two steps before she said, "Ouch," and sat down again.

He picked her up. "Put your arms around my neck," he said. And when she did, he kissed her. She smiled and touched his face, and when he reached the bathroom she said, "I can manage from here."

He went out and closed the door, and when she was ready, after she had brushed her teeth and washed her hands and face, she hobbled as far as the door and opened it. But when she started into the room, he said, "Wait," and, picking her up, carried her back to bed.

He took the bandages off her feet, examined each cut and put more antiseptic cream on them.

"The cuts are better," he said. "I don't think you need a doctor, but you'd better stay off your feet today. After you've had breakfast, I'll send Adela to help you bathe." He stooped to kiss her. "I'd rather do it myself, but if I did, I'd want to make love to you, and the kids would wonder why your door was locked in the middle of the day.''

"Wouldn't do at all," she said.

"Which doesn't mean I don't want to." He kissed her again, and opened the door for Manuela, who came in followed by all six children. The younger boys looked anxious. Four-year-old Hassan took his thumb out of his mouth long enough to ask, "Did you get hurted?"

"I dropped my glass of milk," Kristen said.

"Just like I do sometimes."

"That's right." She took his thumb out of his mouth and kissed it. "But I bet if your glass breaks you're smart enough not to step on the broken pieces."

That brought a smile from both Ahmed and Carlitos. But Antonio didn't smile. He said, "You got hurt last night."

"Only a little," she told him. "Tonight I'll come out to the terrace and we'll all have dinner together."

Carlitos handed her a small red whistle. "You can borrow this," he told her. "Just whistle real loud if you want something."

"I will. Thank you, Carlitos."

Fernando took the tray from Manuela and put it across Kristen's knees. "You children go and play now and let Kristen eat in peace," he said. "I'll be down in a little while, and we'll go swimming. Next weekend, if everybody is very, very good, we'll take the boat out."

"Really?" Even Antonio smiled.

"Really." Fernando tousled the boy's hair. "You can fish to your heart's content."

Manuela ushered the children to the door.

"Bye, bye, Krissy," Gretyl whispered.

"Bye, bye, *amorcita*. I'll see you later."

When they were alone, Fernando said, "The kids are crazy about you." He tucked the napkin into the bodice of her nightgown. "I'd better make sure they're not up to any mischief. If you want anything—" he glanced at the whistle Carlitos had given her "—just whistle."

She gave a low wolf whistle, and he smiled as he went out the door.

Kristen rested most of the day, and that night, after Manuela had helped her dress, Fernando carried her out onto the terrace to have dinner with him and the children.

There were candles and flowers on the table, and red wine for Kristen and for him, lemonade for the children.

"Guess what we're having for dinner," Carlitos said.

"It's a surprise," Ahmed announced. "Because Tío Nando thought you should have something to remind you . . ." He looked to Lucita for help.

"Of back where you used to live in America," she said.

"What in the world?" Kristen asked, just as Manuela appeared, bearing a tray of fried chicken. She was followed by Consuelo and Carmelita, carrying bowls of potato salad and cole slaw.

"And guess what we're having for dessert," Antonio said. "Apple pie à la something."

"Mode," Fernando said. "It was the children's idea. They were afraid you might be getting homesick."

She looked at him, then at the children. Tears filled her eyes. She didn't want to cry; she did her damnedest not to cry. But her eyes filled, and when she said, "This . . . this is so nice," her chin wobbled.

Lucita reached out and patted her hand. "Eat a chicken leg," she said. "It'll make you feel better."

Kristen swallowed the sob that rose in her throat. "Thank you, all of you." She took a deep breath. "This looks absolutely wonderful, Manuela. And yes, Lucita, I will have a chicken leg."

Gretyl said, "This is just like a real party," and nobody made fun of Hassan when he spilled his lemonade.

After dinner, when Lucita went with the boys to play Nintendo, Gretyl took the chair next to Kristen's, and when Fernando asked, "Don't you want to go play, too?" the little girl shook her head.

She made no attempt to join in the conversation. She just sat there, still as a mouse, as close to Kristen as she could get, until at last Fernando said, "It's bedtime, Gretyl. I'm going to carry Kristen to her room now. Would you like to come with us?"

She looked at Kristen. "Is it all right?" she asked.

"Of course. You can keep an eye on my feet, just to make sure they don't get bumped."

The little girl nodded, and when Fernando picked Kristen up, she said, "Be careful of Krissy's feet, Tío Nando."

He bit back a smile. "I will," he said solemnly.

He carried Kristen into the corridor, with Gretyl tagging right behind, saying, "Be careful. Don't bump her."

"Bedtime for you, too, Gretyl," he told the child when they reached Kristen's room and he put Kristen carefully on the bed. "Tell Kristen good-night now."

She stood at the foot of the bed, looking more forlorn than usual. "Good night, Krissy," she said.

"Good night, Gretyl." Kristen hesitated. "How about a good-night hug?"

The child came toward the bed, and Kristen gave her a hug. "Um, that's nice," Kristen said, but when she started to let go, Gretyl hung on, her thin little arms tight around Kristen's neck. "I don't want you to get hurt and die," she whispered.

"Oh, Gretyl, I won't." And though she held the child and whispered soothing words, a voice inside her head warned that she shouldn't let the little girl get this close to her. Because soon she would go away. Because soon she would have to say goodbye.

She held Gretyl close, held her and kissed her and finally, gently, let her go.

For a moment, Fernando didn't say anything. Because he couldn't. Then he picked Gretyl up and said, "Now it's your turn to get carried to bed. You can see Kristen in the morning."

And when they were in the room she shared with Lucita, he said, "Kristen's going to be all right, Gretyl. It's only her feet that were hurt, and by tomorrow or the next day they're going to be well again." He kissed her cheek and sat her on her bed. Then he kissed Lucita and told both girls good-night.

And wondered as he went toward the boys' rooms what he would say to Gretyl and the other children when Kristen left them.

When the house was quiet and the children were asleep, he went into Kristen's room. He closed and locked the door. She looked up at him. "What are doing?" she asked. "Why did you lock the door?"

"I'm going to spend the night with you."

"But you can't. The children—"

"I'll leave before they're awake in the morning." He leaned over the bed. "I can't leave you tonight," he said. "I have to know that you're safe, Kristen. I have to be able to reach out my hand and feel you beside me."

And when she tried to object, he said, "I was so afraid. When I saw Casimiro, when I saw the way he had you, with that knife so close to your body…" For a moment Fernando couldn't go on. "I've never been that afraid, Kristen. If anything had happened to you—"

"Nothing did." She took his hand and looking up at him said, "Come to bed, Fernando. Come to bed, darling."

And when he did they held each other close. In a little while they made love. And in that final exquisite moment when she whispered her passion against his lips, he said, "My love. My dearest. My Kristen."

And wished with all his heart that she really was his Kristen.

Twice that next week, Fernando spoke to the police in Málaga. He had filed the necessary charges against

Casimiro for breaking and entering and attempted murder. A hearing was held, at which Fernando was present. It was learned that Casimiro was wanted in both Granada and Sevilla on other charges. He was to be returned to Granada, and would be imprisoned there.

The whole thing was behind them now, but Fernando and Kristen and the children, especially Antonio, had been traumatized. They needed time to recover, and so on Friday afternoon they set sail on the *Sea Witch*.

Supplies, including a backpack of clothes for each child, along with one special toy that couldn't be left behind, had to be taken aboard the fifty-foot motor sailer.

She was a beautiful boat, white, with gold trim and royal-blue sails. The galley was equipped with a stove and refrigerator and a table big enough for all of them, if they squeezed in together on the built-in benches. There were two small cabins, and bunks that could be opened in the main salon.

Two hours out, both Hassan and Gretyl got seasick. Kristen rushed Gretyl down to the cabin as fast as she could, but the little girl got sick before they could reach the bathroom.

"Don't worry," Kristen said. "It's all right." And held the child's head when she was sick again. She bathed Gretyl's face, let her rest while she cleaned up, then helped the little girl back up onto the deck, just as Hassan got sick over the side of the boat, which made poor Gretyl retch again.

As she held Gretyl's head, Kristen couldn't help thinking, *This* is our relaxing getaway weekend?

"I'll help Hassan," Ahmed said. He ran across the deck to the younger boy's aid, just as a wave hit the boat. It carried them up, then down, and when it did, Ahmed started sliding toward the railing. Before Fernando could turn the motor off and leave the wheel, Ahmed went over the side.

Fernando raced across the deck, grabbed the railing and dived into the water. The waves had carried the little boy almost twenty feet from the boat before Fernando reached him.

By that time, all the other children were at the rail, screaming, "He's going to drown! Ahmed's going to drown!"

A wave broke over Fernando and Ahmed's heads and they heard the little boy cry out, "Don't let me go! Don't let me go!"

Fernando held on to him and started swimming back to the boat. Antonio put the ladder over the side and when Fernando pushed Ahmed up the ladder ahead of him, Antonio grabbed him and pulled him up. Ahmed was shaking, shivering and crying. Once Fernando reached the deck, he said to Kristen, "Try to calm the kids down while I take care of Ahmed."

He picked the boy up in his arms and hurried across the deck with him, leaving Kristen with five almost hysterical children.

"It's all right," she said, again and again. "Ahmed is all right."

"He coulda drowned," Lucita wailed.

"No, he couldn't have," Kristen told her. "He was wearing his life vest. Besides, Tío Nando wouldn't have let anything happen to him."

"A shark almost ate him." Carlitos hiccuped. "A great big shark with long sharp teeth—"

"That's enough," Kristen said.

Then both Gretyl and Hassan got sick again, and she didn't have time for any more answers.

That night, they anchored in a cove just off Torre del Mar. The sea grew calmer, the moon came out, and when the children had had a light supper and were finally in bed, the two little girls in one of the cabins, the boys in the bunks in the salon, where Fernando would also sleep, Kristen and Fernando went up on deck.

He made coffee and brought two cups up on deck, along with two cognacs.

"I thought we needed these," he said with a chuckle. Then, "I'm sorry today was so hectic. It isn't usually this bad." He gave a wry grin. "At least none of them has ever fallen overboard before."

"Is Ahmed all right?"

"Sure. He went to sleep as soon as I made Carlitos stop talking about sharks. Has Gretyl's stomach settled down?"

Kristen nodded. "She was able to drink a little soup, and then she went right to sleep."

"She'll be all right tomorrow. It's only the first day that Gretyl and Hassan get sick."

Two sick children and one little boy overboard. Good God, was it like this every time he took the boat out?

"Actually, the kids love the water. I wish I could do this more often than I do."

More often? She shuddered and said, "Isn't it difficult, though—keeping track of them, I mean? Making sure more of them don't fall overboard?"

"They've had instructions on water safety. Ahmed's falling overboard today was a fluke. Hassan doesn't often get seasick. Part of Gretyl's getting sick, I think, is that she's afraid of water." He took a sip of his cognac. "But water isn't the only thing she's afraid of, Kristen. Sometimes I wonder if she'll ever get over her fears and her nightmares."

He looked at her over the rim of his glass. "You've been good for her. I've seen the way she looks at you, how much she likes you."

"I wish she didn't." She dropped her gaze. "I mean... I mean it's not a good idea to let her become attached to me. Because... because I'll be leaving soon."

A flash of pain seared his insides. He clenched his teeth and waited a moment before he said, "You know that I love you."

She bowed her head. "I know."

"Then why won't you stay with me? With us?"

"I have a company to run, Fernando, people I'm responsible for. I've worked very hard to get where I am. I can't just walk away from it."

"I don't expect you to do it overnight, Kristen. I know that forming your own company was a great accomplishment, and that you worked hard to do it. But you don't have to work like that anymore. If you marry me, you'll never have to work again."

"Fernando..." Tears clogged her throat. She knew she should tell him why she couldn't marry him, that as important as the company was to her, it wasn't only that. It was everything; it was giving up her calm, well-ordered life in New York.

She liked being single, coming and going as she pleased. A long time ago, she had vowed that if she ever did marry, it wouldn't be for a very long time. And that when she did, she wouldn't have children.

Now here was this man, this utterly wonderful man whom she had fallen in love with, but who, God help her, had six children, soon to be seven.

She picked up her glass and downed half the cognac. "You really don't know much about me," she said.

"I know everything I need to know."

"No, Fernando, you don't."

His eyebrows drew together in a frown. "What do you mean? Is there someone else in your life? Someone you haven't told me about?"

"No, it's nothing like that." She twisted the stem of the glass back and forth between her fingers. "My father left my mother and me when I was ten," she said at last.

"I'm sorry."

"My mother died when I was thirteen, and I went to live with her sister, my aunt Mary. When she took me in, she told me and everyone who would listen that she'd done it out of the kindness of her heart."

He frowned, but he didn't say anything.

"She had eleven children," Kristen went on. "At thirteen, I became Aunt Mary's baby-sitter, her housekeeper, cook and laundress. I washed clothes and changed diapers and nursed the little ones when they were sick.

"For five years, I lived in the total chaos of a large family. I was responsible for the children. If anything went wrong with them, I felt, and I was told, it was my fault.

"The older kids treated me like a servant, and that's what I was. I never ate at the table with the rest of the family. I did the cooking, served the food and packed all the lunches and cleaned up after everybody. I did my homework late at night, after everybody else was in bed. I never belonged to a school club, I never had a date or went to a school dance."

He reached for her hand. It lay, cold and unmoving, in his.

"The day after my eighteenth birthday, I ran away. Aunt Mary and her husband tried to make me go back, but I'd had enough of them and their eleven children to last me a lifetime." She took her hand from his. "I don't want the responsibility of children, Fernando. Not mine. Not anybody's."

There was no sound but the gentle slap of waves against the hull. A shadow of clouds drifted over the new moon, and the night sky became dark.

He wanted to cry for the child she had been, and for the hurting child still inside the woman. And for the girl who had vowed never to have children. Her own or anybody's.

"That's why you won't marry me," he said at last. "It's because of the children, isn't it?"

"It wouldn't be fair to them."

"They love you. You're good with them."

"But for how long?" She turned to him, tears stinging her eyes. "I've been with them for what? Three and a half weeks. Anybody can be on their best behavior for that long. Any day now I might start screaming at them, and if I did, I'd hate myself."

"Kristen . . ." When he tried to put his arms around her, she got up and went to stand by the rail. He went to her. "I'd never hate you," he said. "And believe me, there are times when I yell at the kids. I try not to, but sometimes it's a natural and human reaction."

He cupped her face between his hands. "You'll be a good mother," he said. "To them, and to the children we'll have one day."

For a long moment, Kristen only looked at him. "No," she said. "No."

He knew then that he had lost her.

Chapter Fourteen

The call from New York came on Tuesday afternoon. The children were home from school, and they
had just started lunch when Adela came into the dining room to say, "There's a phone call for you, Señorita Kristen."

"Take it in the study," Fernando said.

He had been very quiet since that night on the boat.
He and Kristen had spent the rest of the weekend like
polite strangers when they were alone, like friendly
strangers when they were with the children.

Soon she would leave Spain. In her mind, if not in
her heart, she had already started the withdrawal
process. The sooner she left, the better it would be for
everyone.

If the children were aware of her distancing herself

from the family, they didn't speak of it. But once Gretyl had said, "Are you mad at somebody, Krissy?"

And though Kristen answered, "Of course not," Gretyl had continued to watch her with anxious, fearful eyes.

On Sunday afternoon, they'd sailed the *Sea Witch* back to Santa Cruz de la Palma. On Monday, the children returned to school and Fernando went to his office, where he spent most of the day. Now it was Tuesday, and New York was calling.

"Kris?" Tillie asked when Kristen picked up the phone.

"Hi, Tillie. What's happening?"

"All hell's breaking loose, that's what's happening!"

"Simmer down, Til."

"It's Marilyn."

"Marilyn?"

"That she-viper, that wretch of wretches, that snake in the grass, long-toothed crocodile, that—"

"What did she do?"

"Bought stock."

"In New Woman?"

"Yes, dammit."

"How much?"

"Twenty percent of the shares."

Kristen swore under her breath. "Okay," she said, trying to be calm. "So that'll get her into board meetings and give her the right to vote, but—"

"Terhune's backing her."

"George? George Terhune?"

"He owns twenty-five percent of the stock, Kris."

George. Her right-hand man. Vice president in charge of sales. Something of a letch, but a good salesman. He'd been with her ever since she'd started New Woman.

She tightened her hand around the phone. "All right," she said, trying to speak calmly, "that's forty-five per cent. Between us you and I have forty-eight."

"And Ben Livingston has seven."

Ben. She'd given him the shares, along with a Christian Dior tie, Christmas before last. Seven percent of the shares. If he voted those shares along with Marilyn's and George's, she could lose control of the company.

"You've got to come back," Tillie said.

For a moment, Kristen couldn't say anything. The company. Dear God, she might lose the company.

"Kris? Kris, are you still there?"

"More…" Her throat was dry. "More or less," she managed to say.

"I only found out about it today. Terhune's trying to hold a board meeting without you or your votes. When he wanted to call it for today, I thought Ed Marcus was going to hit him, and so did George. Anyway, he backed down and agreed to wait until Monday.

"Listen, Kris, you'd better get here as soon as you can to try to rally some support from the smaller stockholders. And maybe, you know, maybe talk to Ben."

Ben had betrayed her with Marilyn. Ben, who had been her friend, was once again betraying her.

"I'll leave as soon as I can," she said. "Tomorrow, if I can get a flight. I'll let you know."

"I'm sorry, Kris."

"So am I."

"It ain't over till it's over, kid."

"Sure."

"Maybe there's a way—" Tillie's voice caught and it was a moment before she said, "Let me know when you're coming, and I'll meet you. We'll figure something out. There's gotta be a way."

A way, Kristen thought when she put the phone down. But, God in heaven, what was it?

She told Fernando as soon as they were alone. "I've got to go back to New York right away," she said. "Tomorrow, if I can get a flight."

For a moment, all he could do was look at her. It was too soon. He wasn't prepared. Not yet. *Por Dios,* not yet. He fought hard to control his voice and asked, "Is there anything I can do? Would money help?"

Kristen shook her head. "The only thing that would help is if you owned a good deal of stock."

"I'll call the airline."

"Yes, please."

"I didn't think it would be this soon."

She looked at him, then away. "Neither did I."

"Do you want me to go with you?"

"No, this is something I have to handle on my own."

"We have to tell the children you're leaving."

"Tonight." Her throat felt closed, choked. "We'll tell them tonight."

"It would be easier if I could tell them you're going to come back."

"Easier, but not . . ."

"The truth." There was agony in his voice, anguish in his eyes. Kristen was leaving, and there was nothing he could do to stop her. He thought of the days and months to come, and knew the pain of desolation.

But he wouldn't give up. Because of circumstances, he'd lost the battle, but the war was far from over.

He'd thought before he met her that his life was complete. He'd had the children, and work he loved. Now he knew that in spite of his children and his work there would always and forever be an emptiness in his life that only Kristen could fill.

"The airline," she said, breaking in on his thoughts.

"Yes, of course." He took a deep breath. "Wait here. I'll call them."

When he left her, she went to stand by the window and looked out at the beach, where the children were playing in the surf, all except Gretyl, who sat watching them, the ever-faithful Otto in her arms.

Would the little girl, in time, be able to forget the past, the horror of gunfire and bombs, the deaths of her parents and her playmates? She had brothers and a sister now, and a man who gave her all the love and attention he could. But she needed so much. So much.

From farther down the sand, Kristen could hear the noise of the workmen who were tearing down the old broken piers. Once they were gone, the beach would be more attractive, but in the meantime the noise was nerve-racking.

Fernando came back into the room. "I called three airlines," he said. "The first direct flight I could get was on Friday. I'm sorry."

"Friday? But I have to get back. I have to!"

"I've put you on the waiting list of all three airlines for first class, business or coach. Maybe something will come through, Kristen. But if not, you're covered to leave from Málaga on Friday morning."

Friday. Damn! The future of her company was at stake. *Her* future. And here she was in Spain, unable to leave. She wanted to howl in frustration, smack George Terhune for his betrayal and tear out every hair on Marilyn's head.

"I'll start packing," she said. "Just in case."

"Of course. Is there anything I can do to help?"

"No." She started out of the room, then hesitated and said, "I know this is terribly sudden, Fernando, but maybe it's better this way."

"Maybe." Like death. Did its coming quickly make it easier to bear?

She looked at him and, with a nod, hurried out of the room. Once in her bedroom, she took her suitcase out of the closet and began to pack. She opened drawers, took out panties and bras and threw them into her suitcase.

"Are you going away?" Gretyl stood in the doorway, clutching Otto, looking frightened.

"Yes." Kristen snatched a nightgown out of the drawer. "I have to go back to New York."

"Why?"

"I live there, Gretyl, and I work there, too."

"Why?"

Kristen clenched her jaw. "I have a job. I run a company."

"What kind of a company?"

"Cosmetics."

"What's cos...cos..."

"Cosmetics. My company makes cold cream, different kinds of creams that ladies use. Lipstick and powder and perfume. Things like that."

"Why?"

"Because ladies like to look nice."

"Why?"

"For heaven's sake, Gretyl!" Hands on her hips Kristen frowned at the child. "Why don't you go play with the other children?"

"I don't want to."

"Then just—just go do something else."

"I'd rather stay with you."

"I'm busy now, and I'd rather you didn't."

Gretyl's chin trembled. "Why?" she whispered.

It was the final why that broke the camel's back. And because Marilyn wasn't here to shout at, she shouted at the child, "For heaven's sake, go somewhere, anywhere. Just leave me alone."

Gretyl stared at her, and then, with a muffled cry, she ran out of the room.

Kristen stared after her. "Oh, damn," she whispered, flooded with guilt because she'd taken her anger and frustration out on Gretyl.

"Gretyl!" she called. "Gretyl, wait!"

But Gretyl had disappeared into the corridor.

Kristen picked up another nightgown, hesitated, then threw it down on the bed and hurried out of the room.

Fernando was in the living room. He looked at Kristen, startled, and said, "Gretyl just streaked through here, crying as if her heart were broken. What happened?"

"*I* happened." Kristen bit her lip. "I was upset about the company, and I took it out on her."

"I'll go after her."

"No, I will. Which way did she go?"

"Out to the beach."

Kristen let out the breath she hadn't even known she was holding. "The other children are out there. She'll be all right."

Fernando shook his head. "It'll be dark soon. I called them in a few minutes ago."

She went to the living room door and looked out across the patio to the beach, and saw Gretyl, running as fast as her little legs would carry her.

"Gretyl!" she called out. "Gretyl, come back."

But Gretyl was past hearing. She ran down the beach, down into the gathering darkness of evening.

Suddenly the terrible noise of an explosion ripped through the air. The windows in the house rattled. "Damn!" Fernando said. "The piers! They're dynamiting the piers!"

Another explosion rent the air. Kristen ran out to the patio and down to the beach. She saw Gretyl stop and look up. Then Gretyl screamed, screamed and ran, ran as if her life depended on it through the smoke and flying debris.

"Oh, my God!" Kristen cried. "Oh, my God!"

Fernando ran up behind her. His face was white, strained. "We've got to find her," he said.

Kristen didn't stop to answer. She knew the little girl's fear, felt it, because her own heart beat hard with the same fear. Gretyl had lived through the terror of the war in Bosnia, and now the terror was here.

Another explosion shattered the air, ripped like a bright, hot torch though Kristen's body. She saw orange flame and splinters of burning wood shoot up from the beach, and her mind screamed, *Gretyl! Oh, my God, Gretyl!*

Fernando grabbed her arm. "Wait!" he shouted over the noise. "Wait till it stops!"

But she broke away from him and ran on, ran while the burning debris rained down from the sky and the beach trembled beneath her feet.

Fernando caught up with her, caught her and held her there until it had stopped and the last of the fiery debris had fallen onto the sand and into the sea.

Ahead of them, they saw the workmen headed for their trucks. Fernando waved and shouted, "Wait! Wait!"

Two of the men stopped. "Sorry if the noise bothered you, sir," one of them said when Fernando and Kristen reached them. "We wanted to get the dynamiting out of the way. That's the last of it. Tomorrow we'll clean up—"

"Did you see a little girl?" Fernando cut in.

"A little girl?" The other man frowned.

"Running down the beach."

The two men looked at each other. "We didn't see anybody," the first one said. "What in the hell was a kid doing out on the beach when we were dynamiting?"

"Why in the hell didn't you let any of the residents know that was what you were going to do?" Fernando confronted the men, his face gone hard with anger. "I've got six children. Five of them were playing on the beach only a little while ago. Dammit to hell, why didn't you alert us?''

"Somebody was supposed to," one of them said. "The boss told us he was going to send somebody...."

Kristen didn't wait to hear the rest of it. She started running, jumping over the still-hot debris, stumbling in her haste, calling out as she ran, "Gretyl! Gretyl!"

Behind her, she heard Fernando calling out to her. "It's almost dark," he said when he caught up with her. "We've got to go back to the house for flashlights."

"You go!" she cried. "I've got to keep looking. I've got to find her!"

"Take it easy." He gripped her arms. "We'll find her, Kristen. I promise you, we'll find her."

"It's my fault. I yelled at her. I told her to go away."

"It's not your fault. Kids get on your nerves, and you yell. It doesn't mean you don't love them."

"But Gretyl's so fragile, so needy. I know that, and still I hurt her. We've got to find her. We've got to."

"We will. You go back to the house and get the flashlights, while I keep looking. Bring Antonio back with you. He'll—"

"No!" She pulled away from him. "You go for the flashlights!" And before he could stop her, she turned and started running down the beach.

Fernando swore under his breath. He started after her, but then he stopped, because there was a part of him that knew Kristen had to do this.

He ran back toward the house, jumping over the debris, swearing under his breath at the workmen who'd used dynamite without telling any of the beach residents.

Once in the house, he called out for Adela.

"What is it?" she asked. "I heard the explosions. What happened?"

"Workmen dynamiting the piers. Gretyl's gone, we've got to find her. Get me a couple of flashlights. Hurry!"

Antonio ran into the room, the other children two steps behind him.

"What's going on?" Antonio asked.

"Gretyl was out on the beach when the explosions came. They frightened her, and she's run away."

"Gretyl's run away?" Lucita began to cry. "Go find her," she said, weeping. "Please, Tío Nando, go find Gretyl."

"I will, sweetheart."

Adela hurried back into the room with three flashlights. "I didn't know which one—" she started to say.

Fernando grabbed two of them and gave one to Antonio. "Do you want to come with me?" he asked.

"*Sí, Tío.*"

"Me too," Carlitos said.

"No!" Lucita wailed, flinging her arms around her younger brother. "You might get lost, too."

Ahmed looked scared. Hassan put his thumb in his mouth and sucked hard.

"Lucita's right," Fernando said. Then, to Adela: "Keep the children in the house."

"I will, Señor Ibarra." She made the sign of the cross, then put her arms around the younger children. "We will all say a prayer for the safe return of our little Gretyl."

Fernando, with Antonio a step behind him, ran out of the house toward the beach. It was dark. What moon there was was hidden behind the clouds. He clutched the flashlight tight in his hand. "Let her be safe," he whispered. "*Dios,* hear my prayer. Let our Gretyl be safe."

Again and again, Kristen called the little girl's name. If anything happened to Gretyl, it would be her fault; she'd never be able to forgive herself. How could she have been so thoughtless, so unkind?

Ahead of her in the shadowy moonlight, she saw where the beach branched off in two directions; one direction led to the hotel where she had stayed when she first met Fernando, the other to nothing more than a spit of land. She hesitated. Fernando would be coming soon with the flashlights. Which way would he take? Which way should she take? Should she wait for him?

He would be almost certain to go toward the hotel. Should she have a look at this piece of land that jutted out into the sea for no more than three or four hundred yards? There was a pier here, too, one that the workmen hadn't yet demolished. Though it was broken-down, she'd seen men fishing off it.

She turned onto the peninsulalike beach and started running, calling Gretyl's name as she ran, stopping to listen for an answer, a whispered "Krissy. Here I am, Krissy."

But the only sound was the lapping of the water against the shore and her own panicked breathing.

Ahead she saw the skeleton of the pier. She drew closer. The remains of the broken pilings were dug deep in the sand. Soon the tide would be in to cover them. Water lapped against the loose boards of the broken structure. Surely Gretyl wouldn't have come here. It was too deserted, too ghostly.

It was so very dark, and she wished as she went down the sand toward the pier that she had waited for Fernando. She couldn't see. She should have... Her foot kicked something. She stopped, bent down and saw that it was the one-eared teddy bear, wet and dirty and bedraggled. She picked him up and started under the pier, feeling her way along the pilings.

She heard a sound. "Gretyl?" she said softly. "Sweetheart, is that you?"

A whispered "No." A muffled sob.

Kristen squeezed her eyes shut, held them shut for ten seconds, and when she opened them she saw Gretyl huddled against one of the pilings. Her hands were over her face, but when Kristen said, "Gretyl?" the hands came away and she saw fear in the little girl's face. Her eyes wide, her mouth half-open in a silent cry, she was lost in that terrible place where terrors dwell.

"Oh, Gretyl," she said. "Oh, darling." And then she was on her knees beside the child. She pulled her onto her lap and rocked her. She kissed the dirty, tear-streaked face and crooned soothing words. "I'm here now," she whispered. "You're safe now."

"The bombs," Gretyl said sobbing. "The bombs came again."

"No, they didn't, baby. It was the workmen on the beach. They were blowing up one of the piers."

"They killed Mama and Papa and Munevera and Alija and—"

"I know. I know." She tightened her arms around Gretyl and held her close. "But that was a long time ago. You're safe now." She handed the teddy bear to her. "I found Otto," she said. "He's safe, too, but I think he needs a bath."

Gretyl took the teddy bear and clutched him close to her. "He got hurt, too," she said.

"I know, baby." She kissed the top of Gretyl's head and felt tears of relief flood her eyes. She understood Gretyl's fear now, a fear that would never quite go away, but would hide there in the hidden heart of the child, as would the memory of the father and mother and the friends who had died in the bombing.

A depth of love she had not know she could feel flooded Kristen's body. She would have done anything, anything, to keep this child safe.

She thought of all the other frightened children in the world, and understood for the first time why Fernando had taken Gretyl and Antonio, Hassan and Ahmed, Lucita and Carlitos into his home, why soon the little boy from Ethiopia would become a part of his family.

She thought of her mother's early death and wished there had been someone like Fernando to take her into his home and make her his child. As Gretyl was his child.

She held the little girl for a long time, kissing her, rocking her, and when at last she felt the lap of the water against her feet and knew the tide was coming in, she said, "We have to go. If we don't, we're going to get wet, and so is Otto."

But still Gretyl clung to her, small arms around Kristen's neck. "I love you," Kristen said then. "I love you, Gretyl." And felt the small body relax against her.

She carried Gretyl out from under the pier and started down the small section of land toward the main part of the beach. She'd gone only a few yards when she saw the beams of flashlights.

"Fernando?" she called out. "Fernando, is that you?"

He ran toward her, Antonio only a few steps behind him. "You found Gretyl," he said when he came closer. "Is she all right?"

"Yes, she's fine."

"Let me take her."

Gretyl tightened her arms around Kristen's neck, and Kristen said, "No, it's all right. I've got her."

He looked at her a little strangely, and then, with a nod, he put his arm around her waist, as though to support her, and together the three of them, with Antonio leading the way, started back to the house.

The children, along with Adela, Manuela and Enrique, were gathered in the living room when they arrived.

"You found her!" Lucita squealed, and when Kristen put the little girl down, she ran to Gretyl and hugged her. "Are you all right?" she asked.

"Uh-huh."

"You missed supper," Ahmed said. "We had vegetable soup and chocolate cake."

"I'll just go warm the soup," Manuela said, and started for the kitchen.

Adela stepped forward. "We've got to clean the child up first." She reached for Gretyl's hand. "Come along," she said. "You need a bath."

Gretyl moved closer to Kristen.

"It's all right, Adela," Kristen said. "I'll bathe her." She took Gretyl's hand and, smiling to the other children, as though to assure them that Gretyl really was all right, she led the little girl out of the room.

When they reached the wing where the bedrooms were, she took Gretyl into her own room, and after she had filled the tub with warm water and added bubble bath, she helped Gretyl into the tub and, kneeling beside it, began to bathe her.

"I'm sorry I was cross with you this afternoon," she said. "I was angry at something that happened in New York, and because you were here instead of the person I'm so mad at, I yelled at you."

She kissed the little face she had just scrubbed. "I have to go back to New York, Gretyl, because some not-very-nice people are trying to steal my company."

Solemn blue eyes gazed into hers. "You have to go back?"

"Yes, honey, I'm afraid I do. I have to leave here on Friday."

"That's only..." Gretyl began to count on her fingers. "Only three days away."

"I know, *niña,* and I'm sorry. I really wish I could spend more time here with you and the other children." She helped Gretyl out of the tub and began to dry her. "But you're going to be fine," she said. "Tío Nando loves you, and so do Lucita and the other children. Adela and Manuela and Enrique, too."

She wrapped Gretyl in a dry towel. "Wait here until I find a nightie for you," she said. Going into Gretyl's room, she took a small flannel nightgown from Gretyl's dresser. By the time she helped her on with it,

Adela had come in with a tray that held a bowl of vegetable soup, a piece of chocolate cake and a glass of milk.

"I'll just take it into her room," Adela said.

"No, put it on the desk. She can eat here." Kristen tucked a napkin around Gretyl's neck.

Gretyl had just finished her soup when Fernando appeared, followed by the five other children. "They want to say good-night," he said.

Gretyl looked at them, they looked at her, then one by one they came and kissed her. She looked surprised, but before she could say anything, Fernando said, "Off to bed, troops," and steered the children out of the room.

By the time he came back, Gretyl had finished her cake and milk. "Time to get you to bed, too," he said.

Gretyl looked up at Kristen. She got down off the chair and, moving closer, reached for Kristen's hand.

"If it's all right," Kristen said, "just for tonight, I mean, I thought Gretyl might like to sleep with me."

For a minute, Fernando didn't say anything. Nor did his face show the emotion he was feeling. This was the woman who only a few days ago had told him she didn't want the chaos or the responsibility of children. The woman who had grown up too quickly and who, though she might not be aware of it, still bore the scars of the frightened and resentful child she had been.

"Just for tonight," he said, trying not to show all that he was feeling. "I guess I'll have to tuck both of you in, yes?"

That brought a smile from Gretyl. "Krissy's a lady," she said. "I didn't know ladies got tucked in."

"This lady does." He took Gretyl's hand in his and helped her into Kristen's bed. "I'll sit here with you until Krissy changes, and when she comes back it's lights-off for both of you. *Esta bien?*"

"*Sí, Tío Nando.*" She looked up at him. "I'm sorry I ran away. I won't ever again."

"I hope not, Gretyl. I don't see how I could get along without you."

Kristen came back into the room from the bathroom. She'd taken a quick shower and put on a nightgown he hadn't seen before. He held the sheet back, and when she got into bed beside Gretyl, he looked at the two of them, the little blue-eyed girl, the woman with the soft gray eyes, both of them with blond hair. They could be mother and daughter, he thought. And wished with all his heart they were.

He pulled the sheet up over them. He kissed Gretyl, then Kristen, and in a voice made shaky by all he was feeling, said, "Good night, my dears. Sleep well."

When they were alone, Gretyl reached for Kristen's hand. She yawned and, snuggling closer, said, "Good night, Krissy."

"Good night, Gretyl."

And when, in the night, Gretyl cried out, Kristen took her into her arms. "It's all right, lovey," she whispered. "I'm here, little Gretyl. I'm here."

Through what remained of the dark and silent night, she held the child close. And wondered how she could ever leave her.

Chapter Fifteen

The next morning at breakfast, Kristen told the children she had to leave on Friday.

"But you can't!" Antonio protested. "You live here with us now."

"No," Kristen said, as gently as she could. "I was only visiting. My home is in New York."

"Aren't you going to get married with Tío Nando?" Lucita's chin wobbled.

And Carlitos, his chin thrust forward as though he were facing an enemy, said to Fernando, "How come you don't want to?"

Fernando looked at Kristen. He lifted his coffee cup and put it down again. The children were waiting. He cleared his throat and, with as much honesty as he could manage, said, "There are many things in life that we want to do, but we can't always do them.

Kristen has an important job back in New York. She's the head of a company, and there's a big problem that she has to go and take care of.''

"When she does, then will she come back?" Antonio asked.

"I don't know."

"Will you, Tía Krissy?" Lucita was on the verge of tears. "Will you?"

"I . . . I don't know, dear. Perhaps one day."

Lucita's dark eyes brimmed with tears. Hassan's chin wobbled.

"Why do you have to go?" Ahmed asked.

"Because . . ." Because I have a company to run. Because running that company is important to me. More important than these children? Or Fernando? No, she told herself, but it's what I do.

She had worked hard to get where she was. She liked her life in New York, the silence of her apartment when she came home each evening, an occasional solitary dinner in the calm of twilight at the table in front of the windows that overlooked Central Park.

"Can I go with you?" Gretyl whispered.

"Your home is here with Tío Nando, with Lucita and the boys," Kristen answered, and as calmly as she could she tried to explain why she had to go back to New York. The children watched her: Lucita with tear-filled eyes, little Hassan with his thumb in his mouth, his dark eyes serious and sad, and the other boys, who turned from her to frown at Fernando. And Gretyl, silent Gretyl.

When she finished, Fernando pushed his chair back from the table and headed for the door. "It's time for school," he said to the children. "Enrique is waiting to drive you. Everybody in the car in five minutes."

They left, reluctantly, and when they were gone Kristen went to Fernando's office to call Tillie.

"I can't come back until Friday," she explained when Tillie answered. "It's the soonest I could get a flight."

"Okay, okay," Tillie said. "Ed and I are trying to work on things at this end."

"Have you . . ." Kristen tightened her hand around the phone. "Have you seen Marilyn? Has she been in?"

"Twice." Tillie's voice hardened. "She sailed through the office as if she owned it. Ben was here, too, Kris. He wanted to know when you were coming back. The bastard! It's bad enough that Marilyn is trying to ruin you, but Ben! Damn him! He was your friend, your—"

"It doesn't matter," Kristen said.

"What about the Spanish guy? How do you feel about leaving him?"

"Don't ask."

"That bad?"

"Worse." Kristen's throat tightened, and for a moment she didn't say anything. Then, in a more businesslike voice, she said, "The plane gets in at one, Til. I'd like to go right to the office."

"Sure, Kris. I'll pick you up. And listen, try not to worry. Things still might work out."

Might, Kristen thought when she put the phone down.

* * *

She went into Málaga with Fernando, and while he was at his office she went shopping. She bought presents for the children, games and books and toys, T-shirts with funny sayings for the younger boys, a fishing reel for Antonio, pretty dresses for Lucita and Gretyl. And, because she couldn't resist it, a big orange giraffe with purple spots for Gretyl. Leaving Fernando would be the hardest thing she'd ever done, and when she said goodbye to Gretyl she would leave a piece of her heart behind.

She was laden with packages when she went back to Fernando's office. "Gifts for the children," she said.

"It looks like you bought out the store."

"Just a few things for them to remember me by."

"They'll remember you," he said.

They had lunch at a fashionable waterfront restaurant. They talked about the children, about the food, about the problem with her company. They talked about everything but each other.

That's how it was for the next two days; they were polite strangers who had already said goodbye to each other.

On Thursday night he took her to dinner in Torremolinos, just as he had on their first date. They went to the same *tapa* bar they'd been to before. They ate *bocarones, gambas,* cheese and bread with good red wine. The same dark-skinned man wearing a full-sleeved white shirt with a red vest sat on the same three-legged stool in the corner of the room. For a while he only strummed a guitar, then he began to sing . . .

"Granada, tierra soñado por mi." Land of my dreams...

"Mi cantar..." I sing. I sing of Granada. Granada. Land of my dreams.

A dream she would never forget.

The song ended. "I'll always remember," Fernando said. "I will remember Granada and the first time we made love. I will remember the scent of the flowers beneath our window and the way the moonlight stroked your body."

"I remember the red rose you placed on my pillow."

"How soft you were, how warm."

She curled her fingers around her glass, but when she raised it, her hands were trembling, and so he placed his hands around hers and lifted the glass to her lips. And when she drank, he kissed those lips, still wet with wine.

Desire trembled through her body.

"Are you hungry?" he asked.

And when Kristen shook her head, he put some money on the bar and took her hand. When they reached the car, he pulled her into his arms.

"I told myself we wouldn't do this, that it would be better for both of us if we didn't make love again."

She wound her arms around his neck. "I know," she whispered against his lips. "I know."

They went to a hotel on the beach. When they were shown to a room overlooking the water, he called the house and spoke to Adela.

"The Señorita Kristen and I will be home later than I anticipated," he said. "Please be sure to look in on the children."

"I will, *señor*. I will rest on the sofa in the corridor until you return."

He went to Kristen and began to unbutton the white ruffled blouse she had worn with a black silk skirt. He took it off and put it over a chair. Then the lacy bra. "Look at you," he whispered. "Just look at you." He put the palms of his hands against her breasts, and when she began to tremble he said, "Soon, *querida*. Soon."

She had told herself when she knew she had to go back to New York that it would be better not to be like this again. But when Fernando kissed her in the bar, she had known that this was the way it should be, this one last time.

He cupped her face between his hands and kissed her, deep and hard and with an urgency that took her breath. And while still he kissed her, he fumbled with the rest of her clothes, and his, and then carried her to the bed.

He held her there and kissed her as though he would never let her go. He rose above her, and by the light of the bedside lamp he studied her face. He touched her eyebrows, her nose, her lips, as though he were a sculptor tracing the perfection of his work. He ran his hands through her hair and arranged it on the pillow so that it framed her face. He kissed her lips, and though his body ached with wanting her, he made himself wait as he ran his hands down over her shoulders, her arms. He took each hand in his. He kissed her palms and each fingertip. He encircled her waist and rested his head against her stomach.

Kristen. His life, his love.

He came up over her. He kissed her mouth. He joined his body to hers, and when her warmth closed about him he whispered, "Oh, Kristen. My darling Kristen."

There was a difference in their lovemaking tonight, a terrible yearning to be closer, the desperation of goodbye. They clutched each other's hands, entwined their fingers as mouth sought mouth. And in that final moment, when Kristen lifted her body to his, she whispered a silent "Goodbye, my love," and wept her silent tears.

On Friday morning, she said goodbye to Adela, to Manuela and Enrique, to Consuelo and Carmelita.

And to each of the children. That was hard, so much harder than she had thought it would be. Lucita put her arms around her neck and began to cry. Antonio shook hands with her, and then, with a muffled cry, ran out of the room and down to the beach. She hugged the three smaller boys. They hugged her back, and Carlitos said, "Don't go, Krissy."

"I have to," she said.

And Gretyl, silent, sad Gretyl, looked at her with wounded eyes.

Kristen picked her up. "I'll miss you, baby," she whispered.

Thin arms tightened around her neck, and she felt hot tears against her cheek.

This was hard. Oh, God, so hard.

She put Gretyl down, and Fernando said, "If we don't leave now you'll miss your plane."

The other children followed them to the door, but not Gretyl. She stayed there in the center of the room, where Kristen had put her down. And when the other children waved and called, "Goodbye, goodbye!" she didn't wave, she didn't speak.

When they reached the airport in Málaga, Fernando took Kristen's bags and carried them into the airport. They were already announcing her flight when she checked them.

"You'd better go," he said.

"Yes." But still she stood. Goodbyes were always difficult, but this one was impossible. There was nothing to say; they'd said it all last night.

"Call me if you need anything," he said.

"I will."

"Call me even if you don't."

She tried to smile.

"You know I want you to win. To keep your company."

"I know."

"But I wish you didn't have to go." He gripped her shoulders. "Come back to me," he said. "I love you."

"Flight 557 to New York," a voice boomed. "The final boarding call for the passengers on flight 557."

"I have to go."

He put his arms around her and held her close. "Goodbye," he said. "Goodbye, my love."

She tried to speak, but her throat was too clogged with tears. She touched his cheek, and then, with a sob she could no longer hold back, she turned and ran into the jetway.

He waited until the jetway was taken away, until the jet engines revved, until the plane began to roll down the runway. He waited until he saw the great silver plane take off. Until it climbed high into the sky and disappeared in the clouds.

And whispered her name. "Kristen. Kristen."

Eight hours later, she walked out of Kennedy Airport with Tillie. There was so much traffic, blaring of horns. Taxi drivers shouted at each other, cars with late arrivals jockeyed for position, departing passengers tried to find a taxi or a bus. The gray sky smelled of exhaust and too many people. The air was cold for April.

"I brought the limo," Tillie said. "It's over here."

Artie, the chauffeur, took her bags. "It's good to have you back, Miss Fielding," he said.

"Thanks, Artie."

"Did you have a good flight?" Tillie asked.

"It was all right."

"You look tired."

"I hate to fly."

"You've been crying."

"Yes, well . . . it was harder to leave than I thought it would be."

"Fernando?"

"Yes." Kristen looked out the window of the limo. "And the children."

"But you don't like kids."

"I like those kids." She took a deep breath and, turning back to Tillie, said, "All right, bring me up to date."

They talked business all the way in to the city. Tillie said that she and Ed Marcus had contacted some of the smaller stockholders, many of whom rarely came to the stockholders' annual meeting, and most of them had agreed to attend.

"But I don't know if it'll be enough to swing it your way," Tillie said. "Even if it isn't, you'll still be a powerful force in the company."

"But it won't be mine. I won't be CEO."

"God, I hate this," Tillie said. "I could kill Marilyn for what she's doing to you. And Ben!" She swore under her breath. "It was bad enough his having an affair with Marilyn, but this...this thing with his stock, stock you gave him, is the ultimate betrayal."

"Yes," Kristen said. "It is."

At last they reached the building, on Forty-first Street. Squaring her shoulders, and with Tillie beside her, Kristen entered the offices of New Woman Cosmetics.

Secretaries rose to greet her, and her private secretary, pretty Maude Sterling, hugged her and said, "I'm so glad you're back, Miss Fielding."

Ed Marcus came out of his office to shake her hand and whisper, "We'll lick 'em yet, Kris."

Other executives, like Sam Simoski and Bert Quinn, said the same thing: "We're behind you. We're rooting for you."

She and Tillie went into her office. Annual reports were pulled out, gone over, studied, along with stock reports, sales figures.

"I don't have the sales figures from our Paris office," Tillie said. "Maurice Levesque promised to fax them to me later today, or first thing Monday morning."

Tillie sent out for sandwiches Kristen couldn't eat. She drank coffee, and though she hadn't smoked in over a year, bummed cigarettes from Tillie. It was almost ten before they decided to call it a night.

"Don't come in tomorrow," Tillie said when the cab they shared let Kristen off in front of her apartment. "We've done all we can. Better to get some rest so you'll be in good shape on Monday morning." She squeezed Kristen's hand. "Call me if you need anything, Kris."

"I will." She kissed Tillie's cheek. "Thanks for everything you've done, Til."

"Sure." Tillie swallowed hard. "We've got a chance, you know."

"Maybe," Kristen said.

When she got out of the cab, the doorman of her building hurried over to help her with her bags. He took her into the building and rang for the elevator, and when it came he said to the operator, "You help Miss Fielding with her bags, Richie."

And at last, almost seventeen hours since she had boarded the plane in Málaga, Kristen was home.

She carried her suitcases into the bedroom. She took her shoes off, and her suit, and lay down on her bed. Without thinking, she put her hand out to touch the other pillow. "Fernando," she said, and began to cry.

Fernando called on Saturday. "Are you all right?" he asked when Kristen answered. "You sound tired."

"I was at the office till ten last night." She yawned. "I haven't quite caught up with myself yet. Jet lag, I guess." She looked out the window. "It's raining here," she said.

"Then I won't tell you that the sun is shining and that the children are playing on the beach."

"No, don't tell me."

"I miss you."

"I miss you, too. Are the children all right?"

"They're fine."

"Gretyl?"

"She's..." Kristen heard the hesitation in his voice. "She's been a little quiet since you left."

"Tell her..." What? That I miss her? That I'm sorry I left her? She took a deep breath, and when she spoke again, when she said, "Tell the children hello for me," she tried to keep her voice from showing any of the emotion she was feeling.

They talked only a few more minutes. The conversation was stilted, awkward. Before he hung up, Fernando said, "Call me as soon as you can Monday to let me know how it went."

"I will."

"Goodbye, Kristen."

"Good—goodbye, Fernando."

"God bless."

"You too," she started to say. But he'd already hung up the phone.

On Monday, it was still raining, and there was a chill in the air that belied the fact that it was the first of May.

Kristen wore a suit—gray, to match the day—a crisp white shirt and high-heeled gray pumps. She was ready to leave when her buzzer sounded, and when she answered the doorman said, "Flowers for you, Miss Fielding. Richie's bringing them up."

A few minutes later, Richie knocked and handed her a florist's box. She tipped him, said, "Thank you,"

232 · HAPPY FATHER'S DAY

and, after she had closed the door, took the box into the kitchen and opened it. There were twelve long-stemmed red roses, and a card that read *Suerte. Luck. Fernando.*

She stood there for a moment before she put eleven of the roses in water. Then she took the one remaining rose and, cutting part of the stem off, pinned it to the lapel of her jacket. For luck, for bravery.

She felt the tension in the office as soon as she walked in. All the secretaries looked up from their desks to give her nervous smiles. Tillie, who was on the phone, waved and whispered, "Paris. Their fax arrived a few minutes ago."

Ed Marcus took her hand and said, "Marilyn hasn't gotten here yet, but that friend of yours, Ben Livingston, is waiting in your office."

Ben? Of all the people in the world, he was the one she least wanted to see. She would rather come face-to-face with Marilyn, than with Ben, who for a while had been her friend.

In as calm a voice as she could, she said, "Thanks, Ed," and went into her office. Ben, who had been sitting in one of the chairs across from her desk, immediately stood.

He was almost as good-looking as she'd remembered, blond hair neatly groomed, mustache trimmed, impeccably dressed in a dark tailored suit, fresh white shirt and silk tie.

"Good morning, Kristen," he said.

"'Morning, Ben." She motioned for him to sit back down.

"I wanted to talk you, before the meeting got under way."

She went behind her desk.

"About the shares I own."

"Seven percent."

"Yes." He cleared his throat. "The shares you gave me."

She waited.

"They're yours." He handed a white envelope across the desk to her. "I'm giving them back to you."

"But, Marilyn..." She tried to take it all in. "You and Marilyn."

"That's over. It was over the minute I knew what she was trying to do to you." He stood. "I know I acted like a bastard, Kristen, and I'm sorry. I want to make it up to you. I want it to be like it was before." He tried for a smile. "If it can't be, then at least I'd like us to be friends again."

She nodded and, offering her hand, said, "Friends."

Tillie stuck her head in the door. "Meeting's about ready to—" She saw Ben and frowned. "What in the hell are you doing here?" she asked.

"Ben just gave me his shares." Kristen came from around her desk. "Thank you, Ben," she said. "And not just for the shares."

He nodded. "I won't be at the meeting, Kristen, but afterward, if there's anything you want, anything you need, please call me."

"I will." She handed the envelope to Tillie. "It's going to be all right," she said. "I'm not going to lose the company."

Things happened quickly after that. Marilyn entered the boardroom on George Terhune's arm. She smiled at everyone and tried to pretend Kristen wasn't there.

Ed Marcus opened the meeting and, after a few remarks, introduced Kristen. She touched the red rose in her lapel, then rose and addressed the stockholders. After that, a vote was taken and the proxies were counted.

And when the meeting ended, Kristen was still president and CEO of New Woman Cosmetics.

She and Tillie and Ed Marcus went to the Four Seasons to celebrate the victory. Ed ordered champagne, and they all toasted each other and ordered a ridiculously expensive lunch.

Tillie pointed to the red rose on the lapel of Kristen's suit. "That was a good idea," she said. "It added something special, a display of wit and courage."

"And luck." Kristen touched the rose. "Fernando sent roses. They came this morning." She pushed her chair away from the table. "I'll be back," she said.

"You all right?" Tillie asked.

Kristen nodded. "I said I'd call him when it was over."

She called him. She said, "It's over, Fernando. I won."

"I'm so glad, Kristen. So happy for you."

"I'm having a champagne lunch with Tillie and Ed Marcus, he's my vice president. I wish you were here."

"Yes, so do I."

"Well . . ."

"You'd better get back to your friends, Kristen."

"Yes."

"Congratulations, *querida*."

"Thank you, Fernando. And thank you for the roses. I wore one on my suit this morning. It brought me luck."

"I'm glad." For a moment, he didn't say anything. Then he said, "Goodbye, my dear."

"Goodbye, Fernando."

She put the phone down. "Goodbye," she said again. "Goodbye, my love."

Chapter Sixteen

It rained every day for two weeks, a drizzly, cold rain
that seeped into the bones and chilled the soul.

Kristen threw herself into her work and tried not to
think of Spanish sunshine. She arrived early at her
office and stayed late. She flew to Miami, San Francisco and Dallas to speak to department-store executives. Back in New York, she went to conferences,
entertained executives from her Paris office and received a nomination for the title of most outstanding
woman executive in New York.

She went to an occasional movie or play with Tillie. And once, because she was grateful to him, she
had dinner with Ben. But it wasn't any good; too
much had happened for them ever to resume their
former relationship. When he called a second time to
ask her out, she turned him down.

Fernando called to tell her he was leaving for South America, traveling for Children In Peril. He would be in Brazil, Colombia, Ecuador and Peru. From Peru he would fly to Ethiopia to bring back the little boy he had adopted there.

"I'll call when I get back from Ethiopia," he said.

When she asked about the children, he seemed evasive. She had left them; if he felt they were no longer any concern of hers, she didn't blame him.

Almost two weeks passed before she heard from him again. He called on a Saturday morning. The trip had gone well, he said. Timan, the seven-year-old Ethiopian boy, seemed to have settled in, and was picking up Spanish more quickly than Fernando had expected.

"How are the other children?" Kristen asked.

"Carlitos broke his arm trying to climb one of the palm trees. Lucita is driving him crazy with mothering. I'm afraid he'll break his other arm trying to get away from her."

"And the other children?"

"Antonio caught a four-foot fish, and we're having it mounted. Both Ahmed and Hassan have colds."

"How is Gretyl?"

For a moment, he didn't answer. She said, "Fernando? Are you still there?"

"Yes."

"Is Gretyl all right?"

"She's not sick. It's just . . ."

For a moment, Kristen couldn't breathe. "Just what?" she asked, her voice rising an octave. "What?"

"She's very quiet, that's all. It's like having a small ghost in the house. She rarely speaks, she doesn't want to play with the other children. Sometimes..." He hesitated. "Sometimes I find her sitting in your room with the orange giraffe you gave her."

She didn't say anything, because she couldn't. There was only silence until he said, "I'm sorry, Kristen. I shouldn't have told you. You have problems of your own."

She thought of yesterday's meeting with her top executives and chemists, the argument they'd had over the quality of a new face powder.

"Maybe I could talk to her."

"I asked the psychologist about that. He doesn't think it would be a good idea."

When they said goodbye, she put the phone down and went to stand at the living room window that overlooked Central Park. It was raining and gloomy. God, so gloomy. She put her raincoat on and tied a scarf over her head. When she got on the elevator, Richie, the operator, said, "Going out, Miss Fielding? Not a very good day for it. You could catch cold."

"I never catch cold," she answered.

The doorman opened the door to the street. "Get you a cab in just a minute," he said.

"No, thank you, I'd rather walk."

A walk in the spring rain, to clear her head and help her forget.

Rain drizzled down her neck. She turned her collar up and kept walking. Thirty blocks. Forty. She lost count. The rain came harder, but not hard enough to wash away the vision of a little girl hugging an orange giraffe. All alone, in the room that used to be her room.

She told herself Gretyl would get over missing her. She'd forget that for a little while a lady from New York had come to live in Tío Nando's home.

Kristen walked for a long time, and by the time she returned to her apartment, the chill had settled into her bones. She made a cup of tea and took a bath. On Sunday morning, she awoke with a temperature of 102.

She called Tillie on Monday. "I've got a little cold," she croaked. "Maybe I won't make it in today."

"A *little* cold? You sound awful."

"I feel awful."

"You never catch cold."

Kristen groaned. "That's what I told Richie when I started out on a walk Saturday."

"But it rained all day Saturday."

"I felt the need of a walk."

"In the rain. Great." Tillie sighed. "I'll be over right after work. Until then, either stay in bed or go to the doctor's."

"I'll stay in bed."

In between sneezes and coughs, Kristen slept, or tried to sleep. Hassan and Ahmed had colds, too. If she was there, she'd take the two of them into bed with her so that they could all cough and sneeze together.

Dumb thought. She wasn't there. Adela was a good housekeeper, a nice woman. She'd take care of Hassan and Ahmed.

And Gretyl? Would she know what to do to help Gretyl?

Tillie arrived at six with a pot of chili.

"Chili?" Kristen said. "I thought chicken soup was what you took to somebody with a cold."

"I hate chicken soup," Tillie said as she headed for the kitchen to heat up the chili.

When it was hot and they were seated in Kristen's breakfast nook, Tillie gave her a once-over. "You look like hell," she said. "Not just because of the cold. You looked like hell all last week."

"Gee, thanks."

"You miss Spain, don't you? And the guy, the Spanish dude."

"Somewhat more than somewhat."

"Maybe you could take a week off next month and go to Spain."

"A week wouldn't do it, Til. It would only make the missing worse."

"Do you miss the six kids?"

"Seven and counting." Kristen tried for a smile. It wobbled, but she tried for tough and said, "You know me and kids. They're okay if they belong to somebody else."

Tillie raised an eyebrow. "Eat your chili," she said.

She left a little after eight. Fernando called at eight-thirty.

"What's wrong?" he said when Kristen answered. "Are you sick?"

"It's only a cold."

"You sound terrible."

"That's what Tillie said."

"Your friend from the company?"

"Yes." Kristen coughed and put her hand over the phone to try to hide it.

"Have you seen a doctor?"

"I don't need one. I'll be all right in a day or two."

"I wish I was there."

Oh, so do I, she thought but did not say.

"I've been thinking about your talking to Gretyl. Maybe it's a good idea. I was going to let her talk to you now, but I'm afraid she'd be upset if she heard your voice the way it is."

"You're probably right. Tell her..." She started to cry. She didn't want to, didn't mean to, but she couldn't seem to help herself. Her throat was knotted, and she couldn't speak, couldn't say anything.

"Kristen?"

"I...I have to go. Somebody...somebody's at the door."

"Are you crying?"

"No," she sobbed. "I never cry."

"I love you."

"Me...me too." She clutched the phone against her cheek. "Goodbye," she whispered through her tears. "Goodbye."

The line went dead. He held the phone for a moment before he put it down. He looked out at the beach and remembered swimming there with her. He remembered the sound of her laughter when she'd played with the children. He remembered that first night in Granada, the sound of the *cante hondo,* the click of castanets and the sharp *tac-tac* of the dancers' heels.

"Look how beautiful the moon is," she'd said.

"A Gypsy moon," he'd told her. And later, in the quiet of her room, they had loved each other.

Had he been wrong to let her walk out of his life? But what could he have done? How could he have forced her to stay? The work she did was as important to her as his work was to him. And yet he knew they belonged together. He felt it in his gut, he knew it in his heart. He and Kristen belonged together.

Kristen stayed home for a week, but the following Monday morning she went to work.

"I want to have a meeting in the boardroom," she told Tillie. "Set it for eleven. Make sure all the executives are there."

"A problem, Kris?"

"Not exactly."

Tillie raised an eyebrow, but all she said was "Okay, I'll round 'em up. By the way, I like the blue dress. Is it new?"

"I bought it in Spain."

"Nifty," Tillie said as she picked up the phone to start calling the execs.

At one minute after eleven, Kristen entered the boardroom. All her people were there. She smiled and said, "Good morning. Shall we begin?"

"This is the latest financial report." Gene Miller, the comptroller, handed her a copy. "Would you like to go over it now, or would you rather wait until you've had time to look at it?"

"I'll look at it later," she said.

"I've got the sketches on our new ad campaign." Ed Marcus stood. "Here are the pictures of the new model we've hired. I think she's terrific, Kris."

Kristen looked at the black-and-white photos. The young woman was a knockout. "She's great," she told Ed. "You and Tillie can go over the sketches later."

Beverly Campbell, her head chemist, said, "Here's a sample of the new cream, Miss Fielding." She opened the jar and handed it to Kristen. "Smooth as silk, and it smells like fresh apricots."

"Later, Bev, if you don't mind. I have an announcement to make." She paused to look around the table. "We've done so well in France that I've decided to open up another European office."

"Oh?" Tillie said with feigned innocence. "And what country were you thinking of, Kris?"

"Spain. I've decided to open an office in Madrid." She turned to a man at the end of the table. "Aldo, you speak Spanish, and you know Spain. I'd like you to start working on it."

"Right away, Miss Fielding."

"There's something else." She took a deep breath. "I've decided to step down as CEO."

"What?" Ed Marcus shoved his chair back. "You . . . you can't do that, Kris."

"And I'm appointing Miss McGee to take over in my place," she said.

"Me? You want me to—?" Tillie stared at Kristen, her eyes wide with surprise. "You're kidding."

"No." Kristen smiled. "You'll make a great CEO, Til. And I'm not leaving the company. I'll still retain my position as president, and I'll supervise the Madrid office once it's set up. Until then—" she handed the gavel she rarely used to Tillie "—it's all yours, pal."

There was a buzz of questions. She tried to answer them. No, she wasn't ill. No, this didn't mean she was giving up the company. No, of course she didn't intend to sell. Well, yes, as a matter of fact, she did plan to leave New York.

Finally Tillie, with her newly-acquired power, picked up the gavel and hammered it. "Meeting's over," she declared. "Thank you all very much, and goodbye."

"Nicely said," Kristen told her when they were alone.

Tillie frowned. "Okay, now tell me what's going on."

"I've decided to stop now, that's all."

"And what?"

"Go back to Fernando, if he'll have me."

"You sure you know what you're doing?"

"Oh, yes," Kristen said. "I'm sure." She snapped her briefcase shut. "How about lunch? I'm buying."

"Martinis?"

"You bet."

Tillie put her arm around Kris and hugged her. "Thanks for believing I can do the job," she said.

"You'll be a great CEO."

Together then, arm in arm, they left the boardroom and started down the hall to Kristen's office. Suddenly Kristen stopped. And stared.

Fernando stood in the doorway of her office, a determined look on his face. He was holding Gretyl's hand. Gretyl was clutching the four-foot orange giraffe.

"I want to talk to you," Fernando said.

For a moment Kristen didn't move.

"We've come to take you back to Spain."

"Fernando... Fernando, I..."

"I won't take no for an answer."

"Oh?"

"I'm not going to tell you that the work you're doing and what you've accomplished doesn't matter. It does. I respect what you've done with your company, and I know it'll take a couple of months to arrange things, but I think it's time you stepped down and started thinking about being a woman." He thrust his chin out. "My woman. *Mi mujer.*"

"Oh," she said again. A smile tickled the corners of her mouth. She subdued it. "Hello, Gretyl," she said.

"*Buenos dias*, Krissy."

She went to the little girl and, going down on her knees, said, "I really need a hug, baby."

Gretyl looked at her with sad and solemn eyes. "You went away."

"I know. But I won't go away again."

"Promise?"

"I promise." Kristen put her arms around the little girl and held her close. "I've missed you. Oh, Gretyl, I've missed you so much."

"Me too, Krissy."

"Can I tell you a secret?"

"Uh-huh."

"You're going to be my little girl," Kristen whispered, so that neither Fernando or Tillie could hear.

There was a small indrawn breath, and little fingers tightened on the back of her neck. "I am?" Gretyl whispered back.

"Yes, my darling." She kissed the little girl. "But remember, just for a little while, it's our secret."

Gretyl nodded before she covered her mouth and giggled.

When she let the child go, Kristen stood and faced Fernando. "I've missed you, too," she said. And to Tillie: "In case you haven't guessed, this is Fernando."

Tillie laughed and stuck her hand out. "Welcome to New York," she said.

"And this is Gretyl. Why don't you show her the view from the window in your office?"

"Sure thing." Tillie took Gretyl's hand and, in truly terrible Spanish, said, "That's some kind of a giraffe, kid."

Kristen and Fernando went into her office. She closed the door. "You were saying?" she said.

"That I've come to take you back to Spain."

"Say that part about my being your *mujer* again."

"*Mujer,*" he said with great firmness. "You're my *mujer.*"

Kristen sighed. "You can't imagine how that word turns me on."

His eyes widened. "It does?"

"Oh, yes." She kissed him, slowly, lingeringly. "Oh, my, yes." When he put his arms around her, she leaned back and looking up into his eyes said, "I love you, Fernando. I want to marry you the minute we get back to Spain."

He'd expected to win, but not without a fight. He'd thought he'd have to sling her over his shoulder and carry her out of here. But there she was, smiling, offering her mouth.

For half a second he was too startled to do anything. Then he tightened his arms around her and kissed her with all the pent-up longing he'd had since the day she'd left him in Málaga.

"I'll never let you go again," he said when he released her.

"I'll never want to go."

Arm in arm, then, they went back to Tillie and Gretyl.

Fernando looked from her to the child. He cleared his throat. "Listen," he said, "how about lunch? You too, Miss McGee."

"You bet." She reached for Gretyl's hand again and said, "We'll have chocolate cake with strawberries for dessert."

"Okay." Gretyl looked up. Tío Nando and Krissy were kissing again, right there in front of everybody. But that was all right. Everything was all right. Because she and Krissy had a secret. Because Krissy was coming home with them.

The wedding took place on the patio overlooking the ocean on a perfect June day. The Spanish sky was a deep and endless blue, the sea a turquoise green.

The bride wore an ivory wedding gown and carried a bouquet of pink and white rosebuds. The groom was devilishly handsome in his white tux.

Tillie stood beside Kristen, Antonio next to Fernando. The two little girls, in pink frilly dresses, stood beside Tillie. The four boys, in matching white suits, were next to Antonio.

The guests, some of whom had come from New York, others from Madrid and other cities in Spain, sat facing the sea when the priest began.

"Do you, Fernando, take this woman..."

"I do," he said.

"Do you, Kristen, take this man..."

She looked at Fernando with the eyes of love. "I do," she said. Then, looking first to the girls and then to the boys, said again, "I do."

For these were her children now, to have and to hold and to love as she loved Fernando.

Epilogue

The third Sunday in June dawned bright and clear and so warm they decided to have breakfast out on the patio. Fernando sat at one end of the table, Kristen at the other. Three children were on one side of the table, four on the other.

"Don't spill your orange juice," Ahmed said to Hassen.

"I never do," the little boy said with great indignation.

"Do too! Do too!" Carlitos said.

"That's right." Lucita nodded. "You always do, Hassen. And so does Timan. He—"

"Children." Kristen picked up a fork and clinked it against her glass. And when they were silent she said, "Today is a very special day in the United States."

"What day?" Antonio wanted to know.

"Father's Day." Her smile took them all in. "I think it would be nice if we wished Tío Nando a Happy Father's Day, don't you?"

"Happy Father's Day, *Tío,*" they said in unison. And with a nod from Kristen, both Lucita and Gretyl got down off their chairs and came to offer Fernando a kiss on each cheek.

He hugged both of them, and with a laugh he said, "This is a nice surprise. Thank you for making the day special, Kristen."

"That's not quite all." She handed him the card that she'd asked Tillie to send her.

He smiled and took the card out of the envelope. "I'll read it to you," he told the children. "Here on the outside it says, 'Happy Father's Day.' *Feliz Día del Padre.* And inside..." He paused.

"What does it say?" Antonio asked.

"It says..." Fernando looked at Kristen, his eyes questioning and full of hope. "It says, 'And baby makes eight.'" He stood. "Darling?" he said. "Darling?"

"Yes," she said. "In December." She pushed her chair back and held her arms out when he hurried toward her.

He kissed her, and when he let her go he looked at the children and said, "Krissy's going to have a baby. You're going to have a new brother or sister."

"A sister," Lucita said firmly. "We already have enough boys."

"Do not! Do not!" Carlitos said.

Kristen laughed and moved farther into Fernando's arms. "Happy Father's Day," she said. "Happy Father's Day, my love."

* * * * *

Barbara Faith
just keeps getting hotter!
Her next title,
THE SHEIKH'S WOMAN,
can be found as part of the
1996 Silhouette Summer Sizzler collection.

Silhouette®

SPECIAL EDITION™

COMING NEXT MONTH

#1039 MEGGIE'S BABY—Cheryl Reavis
That Special Woman!
Reuniting with her lost love, Jack Begaye, gave Meg Baron every-
thing she dreamed of—a husband and a father for her unborn baby.
But would their newfound happiness last when Meg's past threat-
ened their future?

#1040 NO LESS THAN A LIFETIME—Christine Rimmer
The Jones Gang
Although Faith Jones had loved Price Montgomery from afar for
years, she never dared dream that he'd return her feelings. Then a
night of passion changed everything—and Faith wouldn't settle for
anything less than a lifetime....

#1041 THE BACHELOR AND THE BABY WISH—
Kate Freiman
Hope Delacorte had one last chance to have the baby she so wanted,
but there seemed to be no prospective fathers in sight...unless she
turned to friend Josh Kincaid. He'd offered to father her child—no
strings attached—but that was before they started to fall in love.

#1042 FULL-TIME FATHER—Susan Mallery
Erin Ridgeway had just given Parker Hamilton the biggest news of
his life—he was the father of the five-year-old niece she had been
raising. Suddenly, being a full-time father and husband started to
sound very appealing to Parker....

#1043 A GOOD GROOM IS HARD TO FIND—Amy Frazier
Sweet Hope Weddings
Country doctor Rhune Sherman certainly met his match when
Tess McQueen arrived in town. But she had a score to settle, and
he didn't want to think about the raging attraction between them—
until the good folks of Sweet Hope decided to do a little matchmak-
ing!

#1044 THE ROAD BACK HOME—Sierra Rydell
When Billy Muktoyuk left home, he impulsively left behind his high
school sweetheart, Siksik Toovak, the only woman he'd ever loved.
Now he was back—and there wasn't anything that would stop him
from winning back her heart.

by Jackie Merritt

**The Fanon family—born and raised in
Big Sky Country...and heading for a wedding!**

**Meet them in these books from
Silhouette Special Edition® and
Silhouette Desire® beginning with:**

MONTANA FEVER
Desire #1014, July 1996

MONTANA PASSION
That Special Woman!
Special Edition #1051, September 1996

**And look for more MADE IN MONTANA titles
in 1996 and 1997!**

**Don't miss these stories of ranching and love
only from Silhouette Books!**